MAKE YOUR PLAY

ASTON ARCHERS HOCKEY
BOOK TWO

CALI MELLE

Copyright © 2025 by Cali Melle
All rights reserved.
No part of this book may be reproduced in any form or by any electronic or mechanical means, including information storage and retrieval systems, without written permission from the author, except for the use of brief quotations in a book review.
This book is a work of fiction and any resemblance to any person, living or dead, or any events or occurrences is purely coincidental. The characters and story lines are created purely by the author's imagination and are used fictitiously.
No A.I. has been used in the production of this fictitious work.

Edited by Rumi Khan
Proofread by Amy Pritt
Cover Art by Essasketch
Cover Design by Cali Melle

PLAYLIST

WE CAN'T BE FRIENDS - ARIANA GRANDE
DANDELIONS - RUTH B.
JUNO - SABRINA CARPENTER
BED CHEM - SABRINA CARPENTER
CLOSE TO YOU - GRACIE ABRAMS
2HANDS - TATE MCRAE
DAYLIGHT - TAYLOR SWIFT
MAKE YOU MINE - MADISON BEER
BLUE - BILLIE ELLISH
BIRDS OF A FEATHER - BILLIE ELLISH
FLOATING - ALINA BARAZ, KHALID

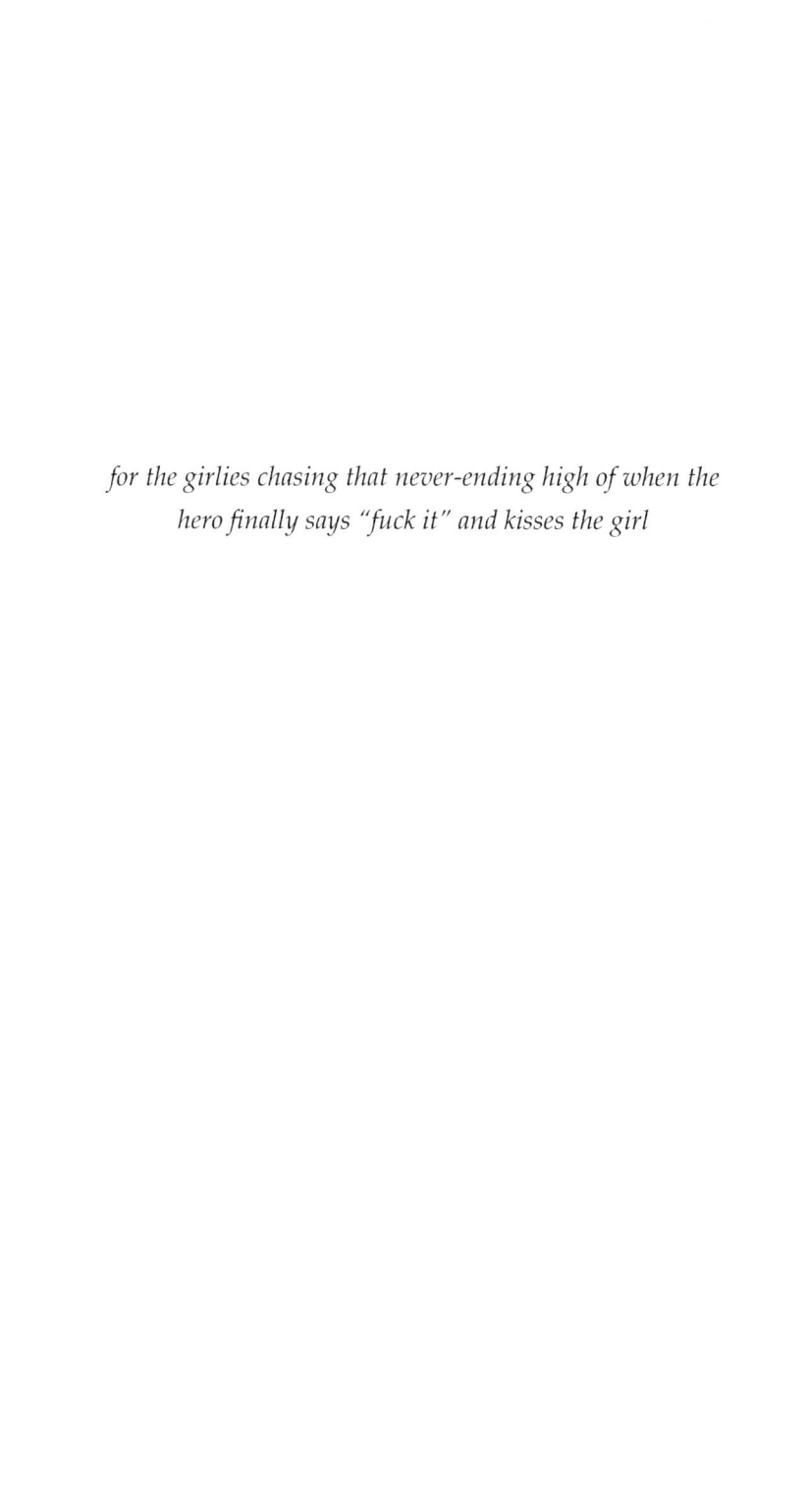

for the girlies chasing that never-ending high of when the hero finally says "fuck it" and kisses the girl

CONTENT WARNING

Please note that this book may contain content that could be triggering or uncomfortable to some readers. It deals with high risk pregnancy, pre-eclampsia, traumatic birth and emergency surgery.

PROLOGUE
NASH

EIGHT MONTHS AGO

I shouldn't be staring at my sister's best friend, but I can't seem to take my eyes off her.

Riley moves her body across the dance floor, holding up the bottom of her lilac dress so she's careful not to step on it. She lost her heels at some point in the evening and now she's dancing around with bare feet. The music pumps through the speakers and I lift my glass to my lips to hide my grin. The cool liquid tingles on my tongue before it burns my throat on the way down.

"You and Riley, huh?" Lincoln questions me as he bumps his shoulder against mine. I glance over at my best friend and my eyes travel across his Armani suit before landing on his dark eyes.

I shake my head at him, pushing away the lingering thoughts of her in my brain. "We're just friends."

"Famous last words," he says with a chuckle as he takes a sip of his own drink. He gives a subtle shake of his head as his own thoughts swirl around in his mind. "Does your sister know you have a thing for her best friend?"

Lifting an eyebrow, I give him a look. "Not sure what you're talking about because I don't have a thing for her."

Lincoln shrugs with simplicity like it's nothing. "Fair enough," he says as he looks out at the dance floor, tilting his head to the side as he watches Nova and Riley. "So, you wouldn't mind if someone else asked her out?"

The thought has my blood boiling. My jaw clenches and I glare at the side of Lincoln's face. His movements are slow as he turns to look at me, and a smile cracks across his face as his gaze meets mine.

"Well, never mind that idea."

His laughter fills the air as Nova and Riley both saunter over to us. Lincoln steps away from me, immediately moving to Nova as she wraps her arms around the back of his neck. He sweeps her off her feet, whisking her onto the dance floor without another glance in my direction.

"I like seeing Nova happy," Riley says softly as she links her arm through mine and rests her cheek against my arm. The top of her head is just beneath my shoulder. She lets out a soft, dreamy sigh as she watches Nova and Lincoln dancing across the floor.

Her hands warm my skin through my dress shirt. "Are you happy?" I ask her as I turn my head to look down at her.

Riley pulls her face away from my arm, her soft green eyes slowly searching mine as a smile lifts her lips. Taking a step away from me, her hand slips into mine and she tugs me toward her as she begins to walk backward to the center of the room where everyone else is dancing. "Dance with me?"

I can't help myself as a smile moves across my mouth and I follow after her.

I don't really dance, but for Riley, I will do anything she asks me to do.

She starts to shift her hips, her shoulders dipping, and we step into the center of the room. We're in the middle of the crowded floor and no one seems to notice us. I don't really notice any of them as our surroundings begin to fade away. The music shifts from a faster paced song to a slow one. Riley reaches for me with her other hand and I grab her, tugging her toward me. She tilts her head back to look up at me as my hands fall to her waist. Her hands are soft against the back of my neck as she laces her fingers together and holds on to me, her body flush against mine.

Her lips part slightly and my eyes drop down to her throat as I watch her pulse moving erratically beneath her skin. "Thank you," she says quietly, her voice barely above a whisper as we move in slow circles.

My gaze steadily trails up her neck, over her jawline and across her high cheekbones before resting on her eyes. "For what?"

"For dancing with me," she says softly as her eyes burn holes through my own. Her plump lips are tinted pink and they move over her straight white teeth as she smiles sheepishly. "I know you don't like to."

"I do with you."

Her eyes widen and surprise passes through them. She leans into me more, enveloping me with her warmth. I could stay here forever with her. My gaze is trained on her mouth as she drags her teeth across her bottom lip. My fingers tighten, digging into her flesh instinctively as I hold her against me. I force my eyes back to hers and I can feel the heat from the flames in her irises as she stares back at me.

"Nash," she whispers, my name rolling off her tongue like that's exactly where it's meant to be. My face inches closer to hers. I watch her eyelids flutter shut, her breath hitching as my mouth nears hers. "What are you doing?"

Something I've wanted to do for as long as I can remember.

"Should I stop?"

Riley pulls back, her gaze meeting mine. There's a mix of conflict, lust, and guilt deep in her eyes. "There's this guy I just started talking to." She pauses, her lips parting as if she's going to say something else. Sadness and regret wash over her expression as she stays silent.

My breath catches in my throat. There it is. The painful reminder that Riley Harris has a life outside of these four walls. The reminder that I have no idea what she's been up to because I've been so focused on keeping my distance from her. She's only here as my plus-one because Nova insisted I bring her to the Aston Archers Gala.

"I don't see him anywhere," I murmur, my gaze dropping to her lips, then back to her eyes. It's an asshole move, but fuck it. I've been watching Riley from the sidelines since she moved to Aston when we were teenagers and she became best friends with my sister.

We've been doing this stupid fucking dance around each other for too long. There's always been a magnetic pull between us, and I've tried to ignore it. I've tried to fight it and I'm tired of denying myself.

Riley rolls her lips between her teeth, biting down as hues of pink dance across her cheekbones. My gaze is drawn to her mouth, watching as she releases her lips with the softest pop. As my eyes travel back to hers, there's an instant ignition of fire in my veins when I see the way she's looking at me.

Lust, want, need.

"I need some fresh air," she tells me, her voice the softest melody against my eardrums. She lifts up onto her toes, her chest brushing against mine as she brings her mouth to my ear. "If you decide to follow me, I won't be upset about it." She pauses, her teeth nipping at my lobe. "Don't let anyone see you."

She drops back down onto her bare feet, her arms abandoning my neck as she takes a step away and spins on her heel. Her dark hair shifts around her shoulders, falling in soft curls down to the center of her back as she leaves me in the middle of the dance floor by myself. I watch her, my gaze following her as she grabs a flute of champagne from one of the server's trays and she ducks out through the back door that leads to the patio.

Pushing past the people around me, I break through the crowd, stopping just on the edge of the dance floor as I see the door shutting behind her. My eyes survey the room, making a mental note of my sister and Lincoln. I almost kissed Riley in front of everyone and didn't think about Nova or Lincoln seeing us. I can't say for certain, but I doubt my sister would appreciate me making a move like that on her best friend.

So, the last thing I need is for either of them to see me following Riley outside.

Caleb and Carson notice me as I walk past the bar and they both hold their glasses up. I grab a drink from a server, making the same motion before draining the liquid in one swift gulp. After setting it down, I disappear through a group of people, slipping out into the cool air of the night.

The patio is lined with lights hanging along the perimeter of the surface. There are two guys standing over to the side smoking a cigar and I duck into the darkness, stepping along the side of the building. Riley's standing along the wall, her head tipped down as she twirls a ring on her middle finger. She doesn't notice me at first and I allow myself the opportunity to absorb the sight of her.

God, she's breathtaking.

Riley's head abruptly lifts, whipping to the side as she sees me. At first, she looks surprised, her eyes wide and lips parted. Her face relaxes, her eyes softening as a smile drifts across her mouth. "Hi."

"Hey," I reply, my voice hoarse and thick with need as I close the distance between us. I don't stop until my feet reach hers and I'm invading her space. There's no hesitation as I plant my hands on either side of her head on the brick wall, effectively caging her in. "You're going to get cold out here without a coat."

She tilts her head to the side, mischief dancing in her eyes. "I have a better idea," she murmurs as she lifts her hands to grab the lapels of my suit jacket. "What if you keep me warm instead?"

There's no hesitation as my mouth drops down to hers in an instant, claiming her lips with my own. Riley's grip tightens on my jacket as one of my hands falls down to her waist. Pressing my body against hers, I pin her to the wall and my other hand slides along the back of her neck. She tastes like champagne—like the stars

She kisses me back with a burning intensity, with a need that rocks me to my core. My cock is already hard, straining against the zipper of my dress pants. The silk material of her dress is thin beneath my palm and I feel the warmth of her body warming my fingers. I resist the urge to tear the dress apart.

Riley slides her tongue along the seam of my lips, desperate for more. Instinctively, my lips part, granting her access as our tongues dance together. She's a whirlwind and I'm swept away in her, tasting, touching, teasing. Just on the other side of the wall is a building filled with unsuspecting people.

The scent of her perfume invades my nostrils and I inhale deeply, savoring every piece of this moment with her. Riley's hands abandon my jacket and she pushes her hands through my hair, gripping the locks as she holds on to me, our mouths melting together. A soft moan escapes her as I reach for the straps of her dress and begin to slide them down over her shoulders.

We're both breathless as I break away from her, my lips trailing down the side of her neck and across her collarbones.

"This is a terrible fucking idea," Riley breathes, her hands slipping out of my hair before they begin to make their way down my torso.

I lift my head, my lips parting slightly as I stare at her. There isn't a single hint of regret in her expression. "Do you want me to stop?"

Riley trails her hands along the waistband of my pants, slowly inching closer to my belt. "No," she murmurs as she undoes my belt, letting it fall open before sliding the button of my pants through the hole. "I'd prefer if you don't."

My mouth finds hers in an instant and a groan escapes me, rumbling in my chest as she slides her hand beneath the waistband of my boxer briefs. The tips of her fingers brush against my cock.

"Nash, are you out here?"

My heart stops in my chest and Riley momentarily freezes. She quickly pulls her hand from my pants and I take a step away from her as she moves away from the wall. Her lips are swollen, her hair disheveled, and her dress is hanging from her shoulders.

I move quickly to fix my pants and shove my dress shirt back inside my waistband just as Carson walks around the corner of the building. He stops when he sees the two of us, his eyebrows lowering as his eyes adjust to the darkness and he realizes what he's seeing.

"Oh, shit."

Fuck.

"Hey, Fordy," I say, the words catching in my throat as I offer him a smile. "What are you doing out here?"

"I came out here looking for you…" His voice trails off as he looks to Riley, who's fixing her dress, and then looks back at me. "I can see I'm interrupting something."

"No. Nope, you weren't interrupting anything," Riley tells him, letting out a soft, nervous laugh. "There's nothing to see here." She looks at me, her expression unreadable, and nods. "Enjoy the rest of your night, Nash."

She walks between Carson and me, her movements hurried as she swiftly disappears around the corner of the building. I don't know if I feel more turned on or more ashamed of what the fuck just happened. I shouldn't have let myself get carried away like that with her.

The silence stretches between Carson and me before he finally speaks. "What was that?"

My eyes slice to him. "Nothing," I tell him, my voice gruff. "It was nothing and you saw nothing—got it?"

Carson stares at me for a moment. "I don't know what you're talking about."

Without sharing another word, I get my shit together and my clothing back in order before we head back into the gala. From across the room, Riley's gaze meets mine. In a crowded room, somehow she always seems to capture my attention. Her stare lingers for a beat before I'm pulled in a different direction, severing the moment, but it doesn't sever the memory lingering in my brain.

A secret Riley and I share.

A secret my sister can never find out about.

CHAPTER ONE

RILEY

PRESENT

Sitting on the couch, the fireplace flickers off to my right and I stare out the window watching the snow as it begins to fall from the sky above. The winters in Aston were never kind. They were always brutal and relentless. The flurries aren't big in size and they're falling at a slower pace—for now. They're calling for at least a foot, but we usually end up with more than they anticipate because of the cold air that sweeps across the Great Lakes.

"Here," Nova says as she steps in front of me, handing me a warm mug that has marshmallows crowding around the top of the cup. "I made sure to put extra in it for you."

A smile pulls on my lips and I adjust myself on the couch, stretching out my legs as I take it from her. She's added extra marshmallows to make up for the fact that I can't have the fun hot chocolate the rest of the adults are drinking. I'm stuck with a virgin version.

I look up at my best friend as she sits down on the base of the fireplace and winks at me. This is Nova and Lincoln's first Christmas in their new house, so they decided to combine their annual Christmas Eve party with a housewarming one. Nova has been bouncing back and forth between tending to Posey while trying to entertain the rest of the guests.

I've been relatively useless, keeping to myself as I wallow in my sorrows on the couch. These past few months have been a roller coaster of emotions and stress. A combination of shitty news from my doctor and being alone for the holidays has been hitting me deep in my chest.

"Hey."

I turn my gaze away from the fireplace, glancing in the direction of where the deep voice came from. Carson Ford, one of the star defensemen from the Aston Archers takes a seat on the couch right beside me. The heady smell of his cologne tickles my nose and I give him a smile.

"Hey, Carson."

He stares at me for a moment, assessing me with his dark gray eyes. "You seem sad. What's going on?"

I know Carson well enough that his assessment isn't unwarranted. I wouldn't go to the lengths of saying we're friends, but more so good acquaintances. He plays hockey with Nova's boyfriend Lincoln and her brother Nash. I know Carson more from association...

And the night at the gala when he saw me with my hand shoved down Nash Simmons's pants.

Such a good look.

"Oh, you know," I start with a shrug, and roll my eyes as I place my hand on my noticeable stomach. "Just starring in my own Hallmark movie. Pregnant and alone for the holidays."

Carson winces, as if he can feel the pain, but he can't. Luckily for him, he'll never find himself in the same position I'm in. "Any asshole who doesn't step up when he gets someone pregnant is someone you don't need in your life." He pauses, taking a slow sip of his glass of bourbon as he looks around the house. My gaze follows his, drifting across the people scattered throughout Nova and Lincoln's home. "He's a piece of shit, Riley."

I tilt my head to the side as Carson's eyes meet mine once more. He's not wrong, but I'm also to blame for this mess. Sleeping with Chad was a drunken mistake I made after only talking to him for a month or so.

When I found out I was pregnant, I really only told him as a courtesy. I didn't want anything from him and wasn't expecting a grand gesture or a relationship. I also wasn't expecting him to tell me he had no plans for a child. He went on to accuse me of it not even being his, so I dropped the issue. I let it go.

"You're better off without him," he muses out loud

as he looks around the room again. His movements are slow and a smirk drifts across his lips as he scoots closer and throws his arm over the back of the couch. "How have things been going?"

"Just peachy," I lie with a snort, a laugh following the sound as I give him the fakest smile. He doesn't need to know all my problems, so I give him the shortened version. "I'm stressed beyond belief, so I'm just going to pretend like things are fine and drink my weight in hot chocolate while I rot on the couch."

"Lincoln will probably kick you out before you fully decompose."

He gives me a serious look before his expression cracks and a string of laughter falls from his lips. I can't help but laugh with him at the truth behind it. After living with Nash, Lincoln seems to be craving some alone time with Nova and I can't say I blame him.

"The floral arrangements you made for the party are pretty awesome," Carson says as he points to the mantle above the fireplace. "Nova said your business is doing really well."

This time a real smile pulls on my lips and I nod. "It is. It was more of a pipe dream when I first started it and it has grown to proportions I never thought were possible."

We settle into a comfortable, neutral conversation, talking about flowers and hockey. It's extremely platonic and I welcome the comfort of talking to him. Carson has always been an easy person like that and his looks match his personality. I've never really looked at Carson in that way, but I'm not blind to how attractive he is.

Carson doesn't notice me staring and I quickly pull my gaze from his face, glancing around the room. Nova is sitting on the floor with Posey, while Lincoln is standing with Caleb and Rowan. As my eyes continue through the living room, the air gets lodged in my throat as I meet a pair of stark, bright blue eyes watching me.

Nash stands by the doorway, leaning against the wall with his shoulder, as he lifts a glass of whiskey to his lips. Another one of the players, Hayes, is talking to him, but Nash doesn't appear interested. Hell, it doesn't even look like he's paying any attention to Hayes.

No.

He's just blatantly staring at me.

I don't miss the way his eyes narrow, momentarily traveling from Carson and back to me. The space between my eyebrows creases the slightest as I study him. The muscle in his jaw tightens before he says something to Hayes. Carson taps on my shoulder, earning my attention again as he excuses himself from the couch and disappears into the kitchen.

I'm left sitting by myself in a room full of people moving about. When I look back toward the far wall, Nash isn't there anymore. An exasperated, defeated sigh deflates my lungs. I need to get myself out of this damn funk. A possible pregnancy complication is scary, but it isn't a death sentence, so I can't let the news from my doctor drag me down like this.

I was first diagnosed with postural orthostatic tachycardia syndrome—aka PoTS—when I was a teenager. As I got into my twenties, it was virtually nonexistent, but my symptoms came back after I got pregnant.

Everything was fine until I had an appointment earlier this week that had them concerned. I've been experiencing some increased swelling in my feet and ankles. The doctors have said it isn't a concern, yet, but they're talking about putting me on modified bed rest, all things considered.

The last thing they want is to have to deliver this baby early. I'm only thirty-three weeks, so ideally, we need more time before the baby comes. I'm already terrified of having a C-section, but it isn't just about it being a major surgery…

The cost terrifies me.

Moving my feet from the couch, I set them down on the floor and lean forward to stand up when I see a pair of bright white sneakers step in front of me. Trailing my gaze along the dark washed jeans and gray sweater, I stop when I reach Nash's face.

He doesn't say anything, he just stares. My heart pounds erratically in my chest a dozen times before he moves to sit next to me. Nash remains silent and I slowly turn my body to the side to face him. The air leaves my lungs in a rush as I find his gaze fixed on me.

"Can I help you with something?" I question him as I lift an eyebrow.

Nash's throat bobs as he swallows. He seems flustered or annoyed and lifts his hand to rake it through his tousled dark blond hair. "Is there something going on with you and Ford?"

"Carson?" I half scrunch my face. "No, absolutely not, all things considered." I let out a soft laugh as I rub my hand over my stomach. My face relaxes as the realization dawns on me. The look on Nash's face when he saw the two of us together… he was trying to assess whether there was anything going on between us. "Would it matter if there was?"

He works the muscle in his jaw, letting out a snort as he shakes his head. "Not at all. I was just curious."

I want to slap the stupidity out of him, but I keep my hand in my lap, wrapped around my mug. "I'm pregnant and by myself, Nash. The last thing I'm looking to do is get involved with someone else."

Something inundates Nash's gaze, but it's unreadable as he lifts an eyebrow. "That doesn't mean anything."

A harsh laugh escapes me and I shake my head. "No one wants to be with someone who's pregnant with another guy's kid. And honestly, dating is the furthest thing from my mind."

"I don't look at you any differently," Nash tells me, his voice soft, warm, and gentle like an embrace.

My mouth and throat feel like I swallowed an entire

spoonful of peanut butter. I'm at a loss for words, completely caught off guard. I want to question him, I want to ask him what he means, but instead I abruptly change the direction of the conversation.

"Well, other people do." I force out a laugh as embarrassment and disappointment prick my skin. This wasn't how my life was supposed to go.

Nash's forehead creases between his eyebrows. "Who gives a shit what other people think?" He glances around the room, doing a quick surveillance of everyone. You're coming for Christmas dinner, right?"

The reminder instantly warms my heart. It's become a tradition over the years that the Simmonses host a big Christmas dinner, where all the strays come to eat. My family moved away a few years ago and I don't always get the time to go visit them. Now, with the doctor telling me I need to take it easy, I'm really in no position to travel.

"Well, given the fact that I'm not allowed to go anywhere, I need someone to feed me."

"Why can't you travel?"

Lincoln suddenly appears in front of us. "I'm sorry to interrupt." He looks at Nash. "Can you help me get Liam's car out? They're stuck in the snow out front."

"Of course," Nash tells him, nodding as he gets up from the couch. He stops and looks back at me. "Are you staying here tonight?"

I stare at him for a moment, my heart beating erratically in my chest. Nash lives two blocks away, so I know he's not spending the night. "I am."

"Good," he says with a satisfied smirk and a nod. "I'll see you in the morning then."

He spins on his heel, leaving me without another word as my head spins. He's kept me at arm's length since the night of the gala, careful not to get too close since that moment. I look down at my stomach, feeling an immense amount of conflict.

Considering the circumstances now, I don't blame him.

CHAPTER TWO

NASH

"Why are there marshmallows in the fish tank?"

I tilt my head to the side, looking at the top of the water as small white fluffy marshmallows float along the surface. One of the goldfish swims toward it, its nose hitting it before it darts back down to the center of the tank.

Nova lets out an exaggerated sigh, shaking her head as she walks over and opens the lid. She plucks all three out and holds up the soggy little balls as she purses her lips. "Posey decided she wanted the fish to celebrate last night. Apparently she didn't understand me when I told her that we don't do this."

Poe comes trotting into the kitchen, her feet almost slipping out from beneath her as she doesn't have her shoes on yet. The small black dress shoes are in her hand and her face lights up as soon as she sees me.

"Uncle Nash!"

Bending my knees, I slide my hands beneath her arms and lift her into the air, tossing her up before catching her. She lets out a high-pitched gasp, followed by a string of giggles as she plants her little hands against my chest. I hold her close to my side, smiling at the warmth she provides, not only physically but to my soul.

Posey was completely unexpected for all of us, but she quickly became the most important part of our worlds. My sister Nova was the best mother Posey could ever ask for and it was amazing watching her grow as a person. I never once doubted her ability to take care of her daughter, but it truly was a joy to see her become the woman she is today.

When I found out about Nova and Lincoln, it was a little weird for me at first. Finding out that my best friend had been sneaking around with my sister took me by surprise. After the initial shock wore off, it didn't take much for me to get on board with the idea. Lincoln knew I would ruin his fucking life if he broke my sister's heart, but that's not something I think I'll ever have to worry about.

He's completely smitten with my niece and equally obsessed with my sister. Lincoln stepped up immediately and he's so great with Posey. I couldn't ask for a better partner for my sister and a better man to raise my niece as his own.

"Merry Christmas to my favorite girl," I tell Posey

with a smile as I adjust her dress around her legs. "Did you already open your presents from Santa?"

"Yes!" She wiggles in my arms, attempting to get down before she points to the living room. "Come look, come look!"

I laugh softly, readjusting her in my arms as I step away from the fish tank, completely forgetting about the marshmallows. Nova walks over to Lincoln as they have some things ready to take to our father's house. I carry Posey through the kitchen, heading toward the living room, when I see her walking through the doorway.

The air leaves my lungs in a rush as I take in the sight of Riley. She's wearing a white sweater dress that falls just above her knees, hugging her body all the way down to the bottom seam. It's fitted around her growing stomach, showing off her baby bump. She's all belly and she's glowing—radiating.

"Hey," she says softly as her green eyes collide with my blue ones. She glances at Posey in my arms and her expression softens even more. The warmth in her irises blossoms as she looks back at me again. "Merry Christmas, Nash."

"Merry Christmas, Riley," I tell her, a smile pulling on my lips as I scan her face, taking in the appearance of her makeup. It's light, just enough to highlight her naturally beautiful features. Her dark hair hangs in soft curls past her full breasts. "You look lovely."

Her smile deepens and she lets out a soft breath that

sounds like a laugh. "Thanks," she says, the dimples forming in her cheeks. "You look lovely as well."

I don't come close to looking as good as she does right now, but I don't say that. I opted out of a pair of black joggers and a sweatshirt and instead decided to dress up for the occasion today. It had nothing to do with the fact that I knew Riley would be there. A pair of khaki-colored dress pants and a dark wine sweater seemed like the easiest outfit to throw together. The tattoos on my right arm just dip below the hem around my wrist.

Posey starts to move in my arms and I smile at her as I give Riley an apologetic look. "If you'll excuse us, someone is being so good and patiently waiting to show me the presents Santa brought her."

"You're in for a treat," Riley tells me, laughing as she waves the two of us on. "Santa went all out this year."

I catch her smile and her gaze one last time before I give in to the squirming toddler in my arms and head into the living room. She practically jumps from my arms and I carefully set her down before sitting on the floor by the tree as she shows me every single thing she got, down to the bows she saved from the presents.

She reaches for my head, sticking one to my hair before smiling brightly. "That's better."

"Much better," I agree, my smile reaching my eyes before I look back toward the kitchen and find Riley watching the two of us.

She's standing just beyond the doorway as she

absentmindedly rubs her hand over her stomach. Something flashes in her eyes and the softest smile is on her lips. Her gaze collides with mine and lingers for a moment before she steps into the room.

"Poe, your mom needs you to come get your shoes on." Riley stares back at me. "Are you ready to go?"

Honestly, I'd go anywhere she asked me to go.

I climb to my feet and Posey breezes past as she runs off to find Nova and Lincoln. I walk over to Riley as she waits for me, expecting a response.

"Let's go, mama."

***

Riley is quiet during dinner and I don't miss the distant look in her eyes as she seems to tune everyone out at the dinner table. After we finish eating, the men are tasked with the duty of cleaning up and I help my dad and Lincoln as we clear off the table and file into the kitchen. We create an assembly line and it doesn't take long for us to finish.

By the time we all head into the living room, Nonna Rose, my grandmother, already has the presents divided out for everyone and she's instructing Lincoln how to help her. I smile at the small stack for Riley. She's been best friends with my sister for enough years that she's practically become another part of our family. Our father always made sure he got Riley something for the holidays or her birthday.

Lincoln sets his to the side and moves down onto the floor before pulling Posey into his lap. Nova hands her the presents from our father and she starts to pull the paper, opening them up carefully. It's not something you would expect from a toddler, but I'm not surprised with her at all.

Posey may be chaotic and a free spirit like my sister, but she has a preference for things to be neat and tidy.

We all move through our gifts, everyone taking the time to open them. Nonna got me fluffy socks and a new bed set, claiming she panic-bought me things because I'm too hard to shop for. My father got me a few new sweaters and a gift card. The last gift I open is from Riley, and I smile as I see what's inside. I take it from the box and lift up the baseball hat, placing it backward on top of my head. I look across the room and catch Riley's eye as she watches me with a wistful stare.

I wink at her and watch the pink tint creep across the tops of her cheekbones. She always used to give me shit about wearing the same hat when we were in high school, so she started this tradition of getting me a new one every Christmas and birthday.

Riley has already gotten through her presents, but then I see the envelope I brought for her lying unopened on the floor next to the couch. I get up from the chair and walk over, dropping down onto my knees beside her as I pick it up and hand it to her.

"You forgot one."

She tilts her head to the side, her eyes scanning the envelope before looking back at me. "Is this from you?"

"You didn't think I would forget you, did you?"

She pulls her bottom lip between her teeth, gnawing at it as she bites back a grin and shrugs with innocence. "I wasn't sure."

"I could never forget you, Riley Harris."

Even if I fucking wanted to…

Her attention drops back down to the envelope and she slowly begins to open it. Lincoln rises up from the floor and starts to take Posey's things out to the car. The night is quickly coming to an end and they're getting ready to go home to get Poe in bed. I watch Riley, tuning everyone out as she slowly pulls out the card tucked inside.

It's a blank one, since none of the cards at the store felt like the right one to get her. Riley's eyes scan the inside and she lifts the gift card up, her brow furrowing as she sees what it is.

"What is it?" Nova questions her from where she's standing with our dad. He's busy putting Poe's coat on for her.

Riley's eyes grow wet and confusion engulfs me as I watch something that resembles sadness and worry mixing in her irises. Her nostrils flare and she swallows before forcing a smile onto her face. "It's a gift card for a prenatal massage."

"Oh, fun!" Nova says with excitement. "They were my favorite when I was pregnant with Posey. It really helped with all the lower back pain I was having."

Riley nods. "I love it." She glances at me, her smile

not quite reaching her eyes, leaving me filled with an anxiousness inside. "Thanks, Nash."

Everyone falls back into separate conversations, collecting trash and their things as they move out of the living room. I turn to Riley, watching her as she moves to get up from the couch.

I can't help but wonder if I fucked up. A spa day seemed like the perfect gift for someone who needs to be pampered and relaxed.

"Hey, Ry, is everything okay?"

Riley glances at me, her smile appearing forced again. "Everything's fine."

My eyebrows lower. "Are you sure?"

"Yes, yes," she says dismissively, laughing quietly as she waves her hand. "It's just the pregnancy hormones."

"I will say, it's been many, many years and I still remember how horrible those hormones were," Nonna injects as she walks up to the two of us. "Riley, can I borrow your florist expertise for a moment?" Nonna looks at me with a knowing smile. "Surely, you won't mind if I steal her away for a moment?"

"Absolutely not," I tell her, nodding. "She's all yours."

I find my father waiting by the front door and I head out with him as we watch Lincoln, Nova, and Posey pulling out onto the street.

"I'm proud of you and your sister," my father says

as his hand clasps my shoulder. "Your mother would be just as proud of you both."

Emotion wells in my throat and I turn to face him, knowing how hard it is for him to talk about her. She was his missing piece and something changed in him when we lost her. It's been long enough now that he's starting to get back to normal, but I know how heavily the loneliness weighs on him.

Riley suddenly walks out with Nonna, my father abruptly ending his conversation with me to talk to Riley. He pulls her in for a hug and Nonna walks with her to the car as he turns back to me.

"I really do hope Mom would be proud," I tell him, my voice sticking in my throat as I pull him in for a hug. "Christmas always sucks without her."

"It does," he agrees, hugging me back before we break apart. "I think she would be at peace knowing we are all happy."

I stare at my father for a moment. "Are you happy, though?"

A sad smile pulls on his lips and the emotion lingers in his eyes. "I'm learning how to be without her." He lets out a breath. "I think I'm going to take that trip to Ireland that we always talked about."

"By yourself?"

He nods. "I think so." He pauses for a moment, like he's choosing his words carefully. "I thought about asking Susan to come with me, but I think this is a trip I need to take alone. In honor of your mother and our love."

He never dated after our mom died, but within the past few months, he's been spending a lot of time with Susan. She was my mother's best friend who lost her husband last year, and she found solace and comfort in our father. I think she'd agree that they're a good fit for one another.

Ireland is somewhere my mother always wanted to visit, but she never got the chance to go.

"I just think Mom would be happy you're going, whether it's alone or with Susan." I nod in understanding. "I get why you would want to go alone."

"I think your date is waiting for you," he says, abruptly changing the subject as his expression transforms into a happier one. This is what he typically does. When things get uncomfortable, he switches it up to cover up the pain.

I give him a sideways glare, narrowing my eyes. "She's not my date."

My father chuckles, shaking his head at me before giving me a devious look. "Right, I forgot."

An exasperated sigh escapes me and I quickly say my farewells to him before stopping to hug Nonna. Riley's waiting patiently in the car. She closes her phone as soon as I sit down and gives me a smile. It doesn't quite reach her eyes and the feelings from earlier are still lingering in the air around us.

She doesn't speak a word and I let the silence

surround us as I head back to her house. As we pull up out front, she turns to look at me, the engine of the car humming from under the hood.

"Thanks for bringing me to your dad's for the holiday," she says with appreciation mixing with emotion in her eyes. "I wasn't sure what I was going to do since I couldn't go visit my family."

This isn't the first time Riley has been at any of our family functions, so I'm a little perplexed as to why she's acting this emotional about it. Perhaps it's just the pregnancy hormones. I remember how Nova used to cry at the smallest things that made her sad or even happy while she was pregnant.

"Fuck," she mutters, ducking her head as she hastily wipes a few tears away. "I'm sorry, I don't know what the hell is wrong with me."

"Hey," I say softly, reaching for her. "Hey," I say again as I slide my hand over hers and give it a soft squeeze. "It's okay, Ry. We loved having you here. We always do."

She lifts her head, blowing out a breath as she gives me a heartbreaking smile. "I know. I love being with you all." She stares at me for a moment before her face crumbles again. Her shoulders jerk forward and she starts to full-on cry.

"Oh, no," I murmur, brushing her hair away from her shoulder and pushing it down her back. "What's going on? What's wrong?"

"Everything, Nash," she whispers, the despair

hanging heavily in her words as her body racks with another sob. "This is all such a mess and I don't know what to do."

Worry inundates me, and dread floods the pit of my stomach, weighing me down like a ton of bricks. My heart pounds erratically in my chest and I stare at the side of her face, desperate for her to look at me. "Let me help you, Riley. Whatever it is, we can figure it out. I'm here for you, and I promise it will be okay."

I don't know if the words I'm speaking are a fucking lie or not, but I don't know what else to do. I don't know what else to say. The way she's sitting in the passenger seat of my car, crying, has panic flooding through me.

She lets out a choked laugh and shakes her head as she smiles through her tears. "There's nothing anyone can do, Nash. I'm fucked."

"Try me."

She stares at me for a moment, a ragged breath escaping her as it shakes her entire body. The tears have slowed down and her sobbing has subsided, but she's still visibly upset. I refuse to believe there isn't something we can do to fix whatever the hell the problem is.

"My health insurance barely covers any maternity care. I've been paying out the ass because of me being high risk and if they put me on bed rest, I'm going to drain my entire savings."

My eyes widen. "Why are you high risk?"

"Because my body hates me." She snorts, another

tear falling. "I started to have symptoms of PoTS again, so they've been keeping a close eye on my heart rate and blood pressure." She pauses, rolling her lips between her teeth to bite back another cry. "They've been a little worried because I've had more swelling than they expected so far."

My brain feels like it's tripping over itself, trying to play catch-up as I'm blindsided by this overload of information from Riley. In all the years I've known her, she never once mentioned any health issues when we were younger. I knew she was pissed when she had to get insurance since she works for herself, but she never disclosed any information.

And she sure as hell didn't tell me she was having any recent issues.

"What are your symptoms? What are the doctors saying?" The words tumble out in a panicked rush. "Are you okay? Is the baby okay?"

"He's fine."

My breath catches in my throat. "He? You found out?"

Riley made it clear from the start that she didn't want to know what she was having. She wanted it to be a surprise and told everyone she'd know what to name it when she met the baby. It was pretty unconventional, but no one questioned Riley because she was always going to do what she wanted to do in the end.

Her lips pull downward as she nods. "During one of the ultrasounds, the tech made a mistake and she addressed the baby as 'he.'" She sighs, shrugging as her face starts to crumble again. "It's okay, it's fine." She laughs, letting out a deep breath as she collects herself.

"What are your symptoms, Riley?"

"If I change positions too quickly, or sometimes just randomly, I get dizzy and lightheaded. It makes me feel like I'm going to pass out and sometimes like I can't breathe. It usually subsides after I sit down, but it's a little jarring."

"Okay," I say, collecting myself as the panic starts to dissipate. My own heart still has a mind of its own in my chest, but it's a steadier beat. Having the information means I can find a solution now. I can fix this for her. "So, we need to make sure you aren't overdoing things."

"I mean, I don't know what the hell to do, Nash." She wipes the tears away from her cheeks. "If I can't work, I'm not going to be able to afford any of my medical bills."

I watch her for a second, my mind running wild with a million different thoughts. There has to be something I can do to help her. Literally anything.

"I'm sorry," she mutters, her head hanging in defeat as she stares down at her hands. "I didn't mean to lay all this on you. The massage was such a thoughtful gift but it sent me spiraling because I don't even know if I can get one with these issues now—"

"Hey," I cut her off, sliding my hand beneath her chin as I turn her head back to face me. Her eyes meet mine in a rush and I brush away a stray tear, my fingers lingering on the side of her face as I stare into the depths of her irises. "We will figure this out, okay?"

"Nash, you don't have to help me. I'll manage."

"I'm going to politely ask you to shut up, Riley." My hand stops beneath her chin. "This isn't up for debate."

"My problems aren't yours."

A smile lifts the corners of my lips. "They are now."

CHAPTER THREE

NASH

"That isn't the hole you're supposed to stick it in."

My brow furrows as I watch Carson with a twinge of frustration. We've been wasting time trying to figure out which lock the key fits into and he has tried the same one three times now.

Caleb whips his head over to look at his brother and me. "That didn't sound right."

"Well, then you come over here and babysit your little brother," I tell him in a huff, running a hand through my hair as I glance up at the clock on the wall. "We've already wasted fifteen minutes on the first clue."

"I got it!" Carson exclaims from beside me as he fiddles with the lock on a separate box. "It was hidden under this other box."

Whipping my head to the side, I look over at Carson

as he opens the box and pulls out a small piece of paper. He reads off the next clue which sounds like a damn riddle.

"What the hell does that even mean?" Lincoln questions us from where he's standing by Caleb. The two of them are trying to decode something written on the wall behind a painting. I'm not sure where the hell they even got the code to decipher what it says.

"I think we are supposed to figure out which letters coincide with the different numbers to figure out the code," Rowan cuts in as he walks over to Carson. Carson hands the paper to him and starts to rummage through one of the other boxes with numbers on the small table.

An escape room was today's little team building activity. The entire team was divided into groups of five and each group was given a different room. Since we're all competitive by nature, everyone agreed we should do it at the same time and whichever team gets done first gets dinner and a night of drinks paid for by the losing teams.

"Listen," Caleb cuts through Rowan and Carson's conversation. "I am not about to lose to any of the other teams, so we need to hurry up and figure this shit out. We have forty minutes left, boys." Caleb glances over at me. "Simmons, see if you can figure out how to open the lock on that door."

Lincoln jumps up, everyone directing their attention to him. "I got it. It spells bone." Carson quickly walks around the table, heading over to the desk where there's a drawer. He moves the letters around on the lock until it ends up popping open.

"Yes!" He opens the drawer, pulling out a notebook that's filled with different notes and poems. "Goddammit. I'm not good at any of this shit."

Rowan laughs, taking the notebook from him as Lincoln and Caleb walk over to them. Carson leaves the three of them to figure it out as he walks over to where I am. I'm halfway through figuring out what letters correspond to which numbers when Carson peers over my shoulder to look at what I'm doing.

"How was Christmas?" he asks as he takes the code from me. We had a few days off after Christmas, but Coach insisted we do this activity to end the year on a good note. I don't think he knew what the hell he was signing us all up for when he picked an escape room as our exercise.

"It was pretty good," I tell him, shrugging as he hands the code back and takes the pen from me to try and figure part of it out. "We went to my dad's and Riley came along with us since she wasn't able to go see her family."

Carson raises an eyebrow at me. We haven't spoken about her since he found me with her at the gala all those months ago. He didn't even question me that night about what was going on because he didn't need to. He may not have caught us in the act, but it was evident we were up to something.

"How did that go?"

I let out a sigh, frowning at the memory of that night. I haven't talked to anyone about what Riley told me.

"As well as it could."

Carson's eyebrows tug together and he gives me a suspicious look. "Did something happen?"

"If I tell you something, you cannot repeat any of this, do you understand?"

He snorts, rolling his eyes. "I keep all your secrets," he reminds me, his voice low as he glances at Lincoln and then back to me. "Remember?"

I cut my eyes at him, not commenting on that. I glance over at the other guys and they're still distracted, so I quickly divulge Riley's situation to him. I don't tell him the specifics or anything about her health. The only thing I tell him is about her insurance being terrible and needing to find a solution to help her out.

Carson frowns as he looks back at the code and figures out the next number. There's only one left now. "Do you remember my cousin Greyson?"

"The one who used to play for the Wolves? What about him?"

"When he was engaged to his wife, she ended up getting a new job and needed insurance because she had some issues going on, so they just got married instead. It wasn't ideal, but they did it on paper for insurance purposes and then just had their wedding after the fact."

Holding the pen against the paper, I lift my head and turn to look at him. "Your solution is for me to marry Riley?"

Carson shrugs, giving me a strange look, like it's not the most out-of-left-field suggestion ever. "I mean, it's not the dumbest idea. We have excellent insurance and it's covered by the team, so she wouldn't even have to pay. It's not like it would be a real marriage."

I chew over his words, handing him the pen again as he figures out the last number. "So, we get married on paper so she gets my insurance and then after the baby is born, we just get it annulled?"

"Yeah," Carson agrees as he unlocks the lock. "It's actually a brilliant idea… if you can get her to agree to it."

"It's not like it would be a real marriage," I repeat the same words to him as I try to warm up to the idea. "It seems simple enough, right?"

He nods eagerly. "Right. You just get married, get her on your policy, and then everything is covered. You can figure out what happens later, but it seems like she needs a temporary solution, and that's the easiest one."

"Did you guys get that lock opened?" Rowan asks as he suddenly steps up behind us.

Caleb is right there with him. "Are you two seriously just sitting here wasting time gossiping?"

"No, we literally just unlocked it," Carson argues back, narrowing his eyes on his brother. The two of them are really close and get along well, but in typical sibling fashion, it doesn't take much for them to be at each other's throats. "Did you figure out what that notebook is for?"

"Yeah, it's for whatever is on the other side of the door."

Carson and I quickly climb to our feet, stepping out of the way as Lincoln opens the door. It leads to another room and he steps in first with Caleb right behind him.

Rowan glances back at the digital clock on the wall. "Thirty minutes, boys!" He looks at Carson and me as he pauses in the doorway. "Are you guys coming?"

"Yeah, we're right behind you," Carson tells him, motioning for him to go ahead. Rowan disappears into the other room, but Carson blocks the doorway before I can go through. "I think you should suggest it to her."

"I don't think it's something she'll agree to, Fordy."

"You never know." He purses his lips and shrugs. "Desperate times call for desperate measures."

Carson slips through the doorway and I follow after him, the idea settling into my brain. Riley is hard-headed and independent, so I doubt she's going to accept my help, but it's worth a shot. It's unconventional. It's not real. It's just a piece of paper that would help her immensely.

And I'm afraid it might be the only real option she has.

CHAPTER FOUR
RILEY

Picking up a rose stem, I slide it into the arrangement, shuffling a few of the flowers that are already positioned inside the vase to make room for the additional one. I take a step back, scanning the flowers as I squint my eyes, attempting to assess whether or not it is missing something. There are a few different prearranged bouquets people are able to buy from my online store and one of my favorites is *florist's choice*.

When they select the florist's choice option, we get free creative rein and at the same time, it's also a fun surprise for the customer. As I look at it, I realize what it is missing. It's an arrangement with red roses and pink carnations, my favorite flower, but it's missing something to balance out those hues. It needs a touch of something white. Baby's breath would look perfect with the combination.

I walk over to the fridge and lift up onto my toes, my arms outstretched above my head as I attempt to reach for the small bundle of baby's breath. My mind quickly fast forwards, making a mental note that I need to order more, when the feeling hits me like a ton of bricks. In an instant, my heart shifts to a faster pace and I'm acutely aware of the pounding feeling in my chest. My lungs constrict and it becomes impossible to take a deep breath. It's a weird thing that's been happening to my body since I entered the third trimester and I know it has to do with my heart and the blood flow.

The reasoning behind it doesn't help to alleviate my symptoms.

Stars dance around the edges of my vision and everything on the outskirts gets blurry. My head swims, my heart pounds, and my lungs restrict how much oxygen I can get into them. I drop back down onto my feet in a rush before I reach for the chair behind the desk. Moving my arms back to the sides of my body helps, but it doesn't take away the pain completely. I feel like I'm going to faint or pass out right here on the floor of my flower shop.

I prop my elbows on the counter, dropping my head onto my hands as I force my eyes shut. My nostrils flare as I suck in a deep breath, attempting to breathe through it to get my heart to calm down. To my left, my cell phone starts to ring and I peel one eye open, glancing at the screen when I see it's Nova. I leave it lying on the counter and answer it, turning it on speakerphone. Words fail me momentarily as I attempt to catch my breath.

"Hello? Ry, are you there?"

My lungs finally expand and I'm able to take a deeper breath. "Yeah, I'm here. Sorry."

"Are you okay?" There's nothing but deep-rooted concern in her voice. "What's going on? Is it the baby?"

I half choke out a laugh that could easily transform into a cry. "The baby is fine." Something being wrong with the baby would be unfathomable, but it doesn't make it any easier that I'm having issues of my own. I never imagined getting pregnant and doing it alone, but this is quite literally the icing on the cake. The fucked-up, falling-apart cake. "Can you come pick me up?"

My best friend doesn't hesitate. "Yes, of course."

Closing the flower shop this early in the day when I have other arrangements I need to do isn't the best thing for my business, but I have to. My body is giving me no choice. As much as I want to power through the day, I know my limitations. I also know the doctor said I'm on the brink of having to be on modified bed rest and overdoing things will put me on the shortlist for that.

"I'm getting ready to leave the museum now, so I will swing by and get you. Are you okay waiting for me?" She pauses for a moment, the concern evident in her tone. "Is everything okay, Riley?"

Rolling my lips between my teeth, I bite down and

nod even though she's not able to see me. "I don't know, Nova. I mean, yes, I'm okay to wait for you."

"I'll be there as soon as I can."

"Thanks, love you," I tell her, my voice barely audible as I end the call without waiting for a response from her. Relief floods me as my heart begins to calm in my chest and I lean forward, pressing my head against the cool counter. My hand instinctively finds my stomach and I slide my palm over my shirt, feeling him kicking inside.

"Sorry, baby boy," I murmur, rubbing my swollen stomach as I close my eyes. "I can't imagine any of this is fun for you either." He moves again, as if he can hear me and agrees. "I don't know how we're going to do any of this, but we will figure it out. You and me, always, little man."

What a mess all of this is, but what a blessing his little life is.

If I can get through the rest of this pregnancy, everything will be okay. I'm a firm believer in things always working out in the end, even if I don't see it at the moment, it will.

It has to.

***

"When the hell were you going to tell me?"

Nova's facial expression says it all, but the disappointment in her voice might be worse.

I lift my head, looking at my friend as I sit in her living room on her couch. "I don't know. I wanted to get things figured out before I told anyone. Your brother finding out was an unexpected accident."

"Nash knows? And he didn't tell me?"

I shrug with indifference, attempting to push away the uncomfortable feelings. "I asked him not to say anything to anyone."

Nova looks like she isn't sure how to feel and I can't help but feel bad for keeping something like this from her. It's more of a private matter and something that hurts my pride. For the first time in my adult life, after working my fucking ass off, in a way, it almost feels like it was all for nothing. Sure, I have my own business and my own home, but what am I going to have when I have to spend all my savings on my medical care.

"What are your options?" Nova asks me as she settles on the other side of the couch. "There has to be some kind of assistance or emergency insurance because you're pregnant."

"I don't think there is," I tell her, my voice quiet as I pick at the skin around my thumbnail. "Because I have insurance, I can't get any assistance."

"I can't believe your insurance barely covers maternity costs." She lets out a frustrated sigh, her nose scrunching as she shakes her head. "There should be a law against that or something."

I let out the softest, most pathetic laugh as tears sting my eyes again. "Unfortunately, there isn't."

"Did they talk to you about what it might cost?"

"Not really. My insurance only covers a small

percentage of things and there are too many variables for them to give me an accurate estimate."

The back door opens and the sounds of voices fill the kitchen behind us as a small pair of feet comes trampling through the room. "Shit. I didn't think they'd be home already." Nova glances over her shoulder, a smile pulling on her lips as she sees her daughter coming into the room. Posey heads straight for Nova, climbing onto her lap before she turns to face me.

"Hey, baby," Nova murmurs, planting her lips against her daughter's forehead. "How was school?"

Posey goes to the local daycare, but she likes to call it "Princess School" instead. "It was good." Posey smiles at her before she looks at me. She scoots across the couch to me, wrapping her arms around my stomach as she presses her head against the bump. "Is the baby awake?"

I smile down at my goddaughter, laughing softly. "I'm not sure, but if you talk to the baby, they might let you know if they are."

Posey starts to talk softly to my stomach, her hands holding either side as she stares at it and then presses her cheek back to my belly. The third time she does it, I feel him move, part of his body pushing against where she is, and she lets out a shrill giggle, her face bright as she looks up at me.

Lincoln comes walking into the room, Nash following behind him. Lincoln walks over to Nova, pressing his lips to the top of her head before glancing at me. "Hey, Riley." He looks between the two of us, his eyebrows pulling together. "Is everything okay?"

My body internally shakes and I fight the urge to break down as I plaster a fake smile to my face. "Everything is fine. I got tired earlier so Nova picked me up from the shop." I look back at Nova. "I should probably get going soon."

Nash stands in the doorway, his arms crossed over his chest as he stares at me on his sister's couch. The sleeves of his sweater are pushed up, revealing half of the tattoos covering his right arm. "I can give you a ride."

"Are you sure?" Nova asks him as she stands up. Posey gives my stomach the softest kiss before she climbs down from the couch. She breezes past Lincoln, grabbing his hand as she pulls him into the kitchen with her. "I can drive her."

Nash shakes his head at her as he pushes away from the wall and steps toward me. "I got it." He holds his hand out to me, helping me off the couch before he takes a step away to give me some space. Nova pulls me in for a hug and asks me to call her later before I let Nash usher me out of the house to his car.

He doesn't say a word until we're both sitting in the front seats. He turns on the car, blasting the heat while he looks over at me. "When was the last time you ate?"

My eyebrows pull together. "What?"

"Food, Riley. When did you last have it?"

My mind plays over my day and I realize it's

already dinnertime and I haven't eaten since earlier in the day. I had an early lunch, about forty-five minutes before my episode. "I'm fine, Nash."

"I didn't ask if you were and clearly you're not." He lets out a frustrated breath as he grabs the steering wheel and begins to pull out of the driveway. "We're going to go eat and you're going to tell me what's going on."

"Nash, seriously," I scoff, shaking my head at him. "I'm telling you, I'm fine. Everything is—"

"Fine," he cuts me off, rolling his eyes as he lets out a harsh breath through his nose. "Yeah, I know, Riley." He pauses at a stop sign, using his turn signal to exit his sister's neighborhood. "Except it isn't."

Emotion hits my chest and I swallow roughly as I glance out the window, directing my eyes away from his. Silence settles around us as I give myself a minute to get my shit together so I'm not a ball of tears in his front seat again. "Enchiladas."

"Huh?" Nash asks as he glances over at me.

"I want enchiladas."

He lets out a soft chuckle, shaking his head at me as he whips the car into the turning lane. "Well, I just so happen to know of a place that makes the best enchiladas."

CHAPTER FIVE

NASH

Riley's face lights up as the server brings an enormous plate of food and sets it in front of her on the table. She does a little dance in her seat, where she quickly rocks her body back and forth, and I can't help but smile as I watch her. Her energy is contagious and it's a stark contrast from the gloomy expression she was wearing earlier.

I know Riley has so much going on in her life right now and it's hard to not let such heavy things weigh you down and poison the other parts of your life. I'm also not sure what happened today, but I have a feeling it wasn't because she was tired. Knowing what I know now, I think it's safe to say it was probably related to her health issues.

"Thank you," I tell the man, nodding as he asks us if we need anything else. Riley smiles and shakes her head, thanking him after me. The man walks away, leaving the two of us alone again, and she wastes no time. "You skipped lunch, didn't you?"

Riley lifts her head, chewing a mouthful of food before she swallows it down. "Oh my god, you were right, these are amazing."

"I wouldn't lie to you," I admit, the seriousness in my tone as her eyes rest on mine. Her lips flatten, parting slightly as she blinks. To lighten the moment, I wink. "I know my enchiladas."

"I trust you." Her lips twitch. "When it comes to your opinion on the best food."

Grabbing my glass of water, I shake my head, moving the rim to my lips to conceal my smile. In typical Riley fashion, she never misses a goddamn beat. "So, are you going to tell me what happened today?"

She levels her eyes on me, narrowing them slightly. "Food first and then we'll talk."

"Deal."

***

Thirty minutes later, we're both completely full and comfortable in our booth as Riley surprises me and starts to tell me about what happened earlier. She tells me about what happened at her shop while she was in the middle of making an arrangement and how this isn't the first time she's experienced it. She goes on to tell me how Nova called, so she listened to her body and had her pick her up.

I'm glad she listened to her body, but my mind takes a more serious turn, playing over the worst scenarios that could have happened. What could have happened if she did faint. If she passed out and hit her head. She was completely alone and lucky that Nova called when she did.

"I don't think you should be alone, Riley."

She cocks her head to the side. "Excuse me?"

"What happens when you experience this again and you pass out? What happens when you're alone and you hit your head or your stomach?"

The color drains from her face and her body falls rigid as she sits up straighter in her seat. "I don't need a babysitter, Nash. I've never passed out before."

"That doesn't mean you won't," I press. Dread fills my stomach at the thought and it leaves an uncomfortable feeling pricking my skin. "You're not invincible, Riley. All it takes is one time and then what?"

There's nothing warm or comforting about what I'm laying out for her to consider. Riley Harris is a strong, fierce, and independent woman. She's stubborn and hardheaded and never asks for help from anyone. "I know this isn't what you want, but you have to think of yourself and the baby."

"Fuck," she mumbles, the word barely audible as her shoulders sag. She lets out a sigh, her jaw tightening as she shakes her head. "Can life seriously stop fucking me? Or at least use some lube?"

"Come stay with me tonight."

She lifts her head, her eyes flashing to mine as she widens them. "Absolutely not."

"I'll come stay with you then."

"No way."

"Riley…" My voice trails off as I dial back the frustration washing over me. "Can you stop being so goddamn hard headed? After the day you had, you shouldn't be alone tonight."

She squares her shoulders, challenging me as she stares at me head-on. "Fine, if it makes you feel better, you can come stay with me." There's resignation in her tone and I'm immediately caught off guard by the fact that she just agreed. "But only for the night."

"Of course," I agree, nodding with her. "I won't hold you hostage."

Though the idea is extremely tempting…

"Well, that's good to know." She laughs softly before letting out a yawn. "Are you ready to go?" She slides her hand over her bump. "I need to get a bath and go to bed."

I smile at her, nodding as I get out of the booth and hold my hand out. "Your chariot awaits."

I lead her out to my car and help her into the passenger seat before walking around to my side. She's pulling her seat belt across her chest, securing it around her body as I get into my seat. I follow suit and start the engine before turning to look at her. It's already dark outside and the lights in the parking lot illuminate her face.

"I think I've found a solution to your insurance issue."

Riley whips her head to the side, her body turning partially as she looks at me. "If it has to do with you saying you'll cover my medical costs or something, I can't let—"

"Marry me."

Her eyes widen and her jaw goes slack. "What?"

"Ford's cousin plays for the league and he did it with his fiancée. She got a new job and lost her insurance and was having some medical issues, so they got married so she'd have his insurance. They didn't have a ceremony or anything before the real wedding, so it was purely on paper so she could get the amazing coverage we have."

Riley doesn't speak. She doesn't say a fucking word. She just stares at me with that same shocked expression. Anticipation swirls in the pit of my stomach and I don't even know why. I'm not asking her to marry me for real. It's just to help her out while she's in a shitty position.

"Nash, isn't that insurance fraud?"

I can't help myself as I laugh. "Really? That's your response?"

Insurance fraud is something I thought about when first thinking of the idea, but really, there's no way for anyone to prove that it's fraud. And technically, she's not marrying me for my insurance without me knowing. She's not at fault if I'm the one who's proposing the entire idea.

"I mean, that's a legitimate concern," she snaps at

me, her energy not matching mine. I can't tell if she's annoyed or pissed off or what the hell happened, but she's not laughing. "I'm not going to do something that could get you in trouble."

Her words catch me by surprise. "Wait, you're considering it?"

"I didn't say that," she tells me, shaking her head. "I'm just saying, I wouldn't ever do anything that could possibly get you in trouble. And I already told you, I'm not letting you pay for my insurance."

"It's covered by the organization," I explain to her, not completely sure how it works for spouses, but what she doesn't know won't hurt her.

She's silent as her eyes roam across my face. "So, you want to come stay with me tonight and you want me to marry you?"

"It's all just temporary," I tell her, stressing the point she tried to make earlier when I told her to come stay with me. "After the baby is born, we can get an annulment."

I cannot believe she's actually considering this.

"I can't believe I'm really giving this any thought right now." She pauses, letting out a breathy laugh as she shakes her head. "If we do this, I don't want anyone to know."

"Of course not," I assure her, nodding convincingly. "It won't be real. It will just be on paper for the insurance."

"This is crazy, Nash," she says, her eyes wide. "I don't even know what to say to this right now."

"You don't have to decide right now," I tell her as I begin to pull the car from the parking lot to head to her house. "I just want you to know you have other options and this one doesn't involve me paying for it." I pause, my foot pressing on the brakes as I glance over at her. "You are going to have to do something soon, Riley."

Her throat bobs as she swallows. "I know."

She's quiet for most of the ride back to her house and I don't push the issue. This is a decision Riley has to make herself, but she knows she's out of options. She has to know this is her best one, but I don't want to press her on it. I don't want to make her feel pressured or forced.

I just want her to be okay.

I want her to say she's fine—that everything is fine—and have it be the truth.

I want her to let me help her.

***

"I'll show you where you can sleep so you don't have to sleep on the couch."

"I don't mind the couch," I say, bowing my head as I sweep my arm toward the door. Riley snorts, ducking her head to conceal her smile as she walks to the bottom of the stairs. She turns to glance at me, giving me a look that says I'd better follow her. "Yes, ma'am. Let's go."

We reach the second floor and she motions toward the bathroom. "I know you've been in here before, but in case you forgot, the bathroom is over there." She pauses, a sheepish grin playing on her lips. "There should be an extra toothbrush you can use."

"Slow down, babe," I tell her, my voice soft as I wink at her. "I didn't think things would move this fast."

Riley whips her head to the side, staring at me with her eyes wide and a blank look on her face. "But you just asked me to marry you."

I stare back at her for a moment before my face cracks and laughter spills from my lips. Riley's face lights up and the soft sound of her laughing dances across my eardrums. Even if it's only for a short moment, I like her like this—not worried about everything else that is going on in life.

If I can help ease her burdens and worries, just to see her like this, I'll do whatever the fuck I have to.

"Okay, the guest room is over here," Riley tells me as she walks past two other doors and stops at the one on the right. She opens the door, pushing it as we step inside. There's a king-sized bed along the far wall, jutting out into the center of the room. Across from it is a dresser with a TV mounted on the wall above. The left wall is all windows and the right is a big walk-in closet.

"I really would have been fine with the couch," I say, glancing around at all the space. Riley watches me as I walk to the windows, glancing out at the backyard. Turning back around, I look out into the hall and then back to her. "Which room is going to be the baby's?"

"The one across the hall." She glances over her shoulder and back to me. "It's not finished and I still have a few things left to do."

"Can I see it?"

A nervousness sweeps across her face. "I guess. It's not ready yet, so keep that in mind."

Riley spins on her heel and I follow her to the room across from mine. She pushes open the door and I'm half expecting to see it looking like the rest of her house, except it doesn't. The walls are white and it's barren. There's a small dark gray rug in the center and a few boxes.

"Nova told me I should wait to order stuff until after the baby shower, so there's not much yet." She turns back to me, shrugging her shoulders. "I did order a crib and a dresser, but they won't be here for a few more weeks because the set I picked was on backorder." She pauses, looking at the wall before letting out a sigh. "I need to paint too."

"I don't think you're supposed to do that when you're pregnant," I say, remembering how I painted for Nova when she was pregnant.

Her throat bobs as she swallows. "Yeah, I don't know. I thought if I wore one of those masks, I could get it done."

I stare at her for a moment, irritation pricking my skin. "I'll do it."

"Nash, no. I can't ask you to do that. You're already doing too much."

"You're not asking," I tell her, the muscle in my jaw tightening as I push my hands into the front pockets of my pants. "I'm telling you I will do it. I want to do it, so please, just let me paint the fucking room for you." I let out a frustrated sigh. "I'm sorry, that came out wrong. I know you are independent and you don't need any help, but I am begging you to please let me, Riley."

She looks unsure at first, but finally she nods. "Okay, you're right. I shouldn't be painting."

"There are a lot of things you probably shouldn't be doing, but one step at a time."

"One step at a time," she repeats, nodding as her eyes search mine. Her lips part, as if she's going to say something else, but she quickly shuts them again.

I would give anything to know what's going on in that head of hers, but I'll settle with what she gives me for now.

CHAPTER SIX

RILEY

I can't believe I am actually contemplating marrying him.

It's almost as if he found a loophole to help me, but technically he isn't paying directly out of pocket for the insurance, so that's supposed to make it better. A part of me thinks maybe I should just let him pay for it, but then I don't want to feel like I owe him. If I marry him, it's a piece of paper. A legal binding that ties me to him in that sense. No one has to know. It can be our secret and like he said, after the baby is born, I won't have a use for it. I can get everything else figured out and we can get the marriage annulled.

It's not like we'd ever consummate the marriage anyway…

It seems pretty simple, like it's the easiest option I have, and it's starting to feel like I don't have any other real viable ones at this point.

The only thing is, if we do this, no one can ever know. There's a part of me that feels ashamed for considering marrying him for his insurance even if it is a mutual decision. Nash won't be blindsided by any of this and he's the one who proposed it in the first place. But even still, there's a weird feeling that comes along with it.

My phone rings on my nightstand and I roll over in bed, grabbing it as I find a small piece of paper. I answer the call as my eyes scan the note.

"Hey."

I didn't want to wake you when I left, but text me after you're up so I know you're okay.
Nash

"What are you doing?" Nova asks me with no sense of worry or concern in her tone. "How are you feeling?"

"Better," I tell her with a smile on my lips as I walk to my closet to pick out an outfit for the day. I planned on it being a slower day, opening the flower shop closer to late morning to give myself some time. "Nash took me to get dinner, which seemed to help, and then I slept for at least ten hours last night."

"I heard Nash stayed over last night."

My stomach instantly drops. "Did you talk to him?" I don't know what the hell he would have said to her and I can't help but hope he didn't say anything about the marriage.

"He called me, like, five minutes ago."

Maybe he didn't bring up the arrangement.

"Yeah, he said he didn't think I should be alone." I let out a nervous laugh. "Honestly, the company was nice."

"I agree with him, Ry. Yesterday was scary and the thought of you being home alone makes me nervous."

My phone vibrates and I pull it away from my ear, putting the call on speakerphone as I check my messages.

> NASH
>
> Are you awake yet?
>
> NASH
>
> I hope you're feeling better this morning.

A smile pulls on my lips at his lack of patience and double texts.

> RILEY
>
> Definitely better today. Thanks for staying last night.
>
> NASH
>
> Whatever you need, I'm here.
>
> RILEY
>
> Actually, I was wondering if we could maybe talk again, if you're free anytime soon.
>
> NASH
>
> Does 6 or 7 tonight work for you?

> **RILEY**
> Sure, that's fine. Are you planning on eating dinner before coming or should I make something?

> **NASH**
> Don't make anything.
>
> But wait for me to eat.

> **RILEY**
> What are you up to, Simmons?

> **NASH**
> You'll see ;) I promise you'll like it though.

"Riley Lynn Harris. Are you alive?"

"Sorry, sorry." I laugh, shaking my head. "I got distracted, but I'm here."

"What the hell happened?"

Oh, you know, your brother, who told me to marry him to solve my problems, wants to come over later.

It's on the tip of my tongue to say something to her about his proposal, but I clamp my lips shut and swallow back my words.

What a fucking situation I've gotten myself into.

"It's okay, it happens to me all the time." She pauses and I hear muffled voices in the background. "Ope, I hate to call and hang up, but I need to get back to work. I'm currently getting the stink eye from management. Love you!"

"Love you too!"

As I end the call with Nova, my stomach shifts and I feel my little guy moving around. My heart swells in my chest and my hand instinctively finds my belly. There's no use in fighting the smile that tugs my lips upwards. He moves again, his little foot kicking my hand. He's right on track with where he's supposed to be growth-wise. We've had no issues with him, it's only been my health, but if something happens to me, he's also in jeopardy.

I need to be here for him after he makes his entrance into the world.

I have to marry Nash Simmons.

It's the only way to ensure things go smoothly and I'm not stuck with a six-figure hospital bill.

I have to marry my best friend's brother.

***

It's exactly six-fifteen when a soft knock sounds from my front door. I climb off the couch, walking over to unlock the door and let him in. As I pull the door open, I find Nash with a few grocery bags in his hands. My eyes drop down to them before landing on his blue eyes. "Hi. What is all this?"

"I told you not to worry about dinner," he says with a smile as I move out of his way and he steps into the house. "I stopped and grabbed some things so I could cook for you." He smirks. "Okay, we know I'm not a good cook. I grabbed some food to heat up."

I stand out of the way, watching Nash as he walks into my home like this is exactly where he's supposed to be. His presence is demanding and he fills the space. He knows his way around my house and he walks directly into the kitchen. The rustling of the plastic bags comes from the counter, and I pause in the doorway as I watch him again.

"I was going to make shrimp scampi with pasta. I know you've been on an enchilada kick, but if I remember correctly, shrimp scampi is one of your favorites."

My breath catches in my throat, my chest constricting. "It is. How did you know that?"

"I've known you long enough, Riley. I'd be a terrible friend if I didn't know your favorites."

I narrow my eyes at him, walking across the kitchen before pulling out one of the stools at the island. "What's my favorite color?"

"Easy. Purple."

"Favorite season?"

He grabs the pots and skillet and looks at me with a smirk. "Hockey, duh." He lets out a chuckle. "Kidding. You're a summer girl." He starts to get everything prepped and turns around to face me. "Your favorite book series is Harry Potter. You live for holiday Hallmark movies. You're not a big fan of flip-flops, but you'll wear those over sandals. Is there anything else you'd like to quiz me on?"

I'm momentarily speechless. I don't remember ever

intentionally telling him any of this, but it's like he's stored these small details about me inside his brain for safekeeping. "How do you remember all this?"

His lips part, something unreadable engulfing his eyes before his tongue darts out to wet his lips instead. His nostrils flare and his voice drops a touch. "I pay attention, Riley." His gaze lingers and he begins to turn around to heat up the food when I blurt out the words.

"I'll do it."

He tilts his head to the side, his eyebrows scrunching together. "Do what?"

"I'll marry you." I let out a nervous breath, adjusting on the stool as his face lights up. "For your insurance."

Tension hangs heavily in the air between us and it's borderline suffocating. Under his gaze, I feel like I need to change into a t-shirt with how flushed my body feels. Nash stares at me with an intensity that sends wildfire through my veins. "Good," he says slowly with a nod. "It's the best option you have and I promise you, no one will ever have to know."

"Thank you," I half whisper, my voice getting caught in my throat as emotion engulfs me. "Not just for this, but for everything."

"You don't have to thank me."

"But I do," I explain as I lean against the counter, watching him as he turns around to dump the contents from the container into a pan. "You never judge and you never hesitate. You're always there for me, literally through everything."

He looks back at me, his gaze colliding with mine. "I'm not going anywhere," he promises, his eyes burning holes through mine. "I'll always be here."

In a different life, it could have been us… but not in this one.

CHAPTER SEVEN

NASH

The puck slides across the ice as I push it with the blade of my stick, skating through two players, dodging their hits as I head toward the net. I'm on a breakaway and I can't see any of their defense getting close to me. Carson yells my name from the left and I glance at him from the corner of my eye, still keeping my direct attention on the net and the goalie who's bending his knees, getting into position.

"To your right, Nash!"

As the words fall from Carson's lips, I quickly try to look to the left as a stick reaches toward mine. Pushing my legs harder, I pass the puck to Carson, knowing it's a safer move than trying to keep possession of the puck myself. The player on my heels manages to hook my stick and jerks it toward him, trying to pull it from my grip.

Carson shoots and the goalie lifts his glove to block

the top-left corner, catching it effortlessly. Turning my feet to the side, I come to an abrupt stop, the blades of my skates cutting into the ice. My stick escapes the asshole who was trying to disarm me. As he skates past, he moves toward me, his shoulder coming right for mine. I don't move and instead hold my ground, letting him hit me.

I grab the back of his jersey, jerking him back toward me when the ref rushes over and immediately pushes me away from him. I lock eyes with the other winger. Number 21. Collins. "We're not done here."

He grins at me, a gap showing in his teeth as he winks. "See you next shift, Simmons."

"Nash, hurry the fuck up!"

I glance over at the bench and find Hayes glaring at me while everyone else already switched and is skating over to the face-off dot. My feet move quickly and I head back to the bench, climbing over the boards as he skates over to where they're waiting.

"What the hell was that?" Lincoln questions me as he wipes the fog from his helmet visor. "Did something happen between you and Collins again?"

Again—funny he should use that word. Eli Collins and I have a history of not getting along after he tried to date my sister when she was in college. I shake my head, lifting a bottle to squirt water into my mouth as I watch play start on the ice again. "I hit him pretty hard during the first period. He's been coming for me since then."

"Well, you know what you have to do," Carson chimes in from where he's sitting farther down the bench. "Give him what he wants."

"He wants to fight."

Carson gives me a playful grin with mischief dancing in his gray eyes. "Exactly."

I shake my head, glancing back at the ice as I watch our guys fighting for a goal. We're down by two going into the third period and if this ends up being a shutout, we're all going to get ripped a new one by Coach. No one likes a shutout, especially him.

There's only five minutes left in the third period and things are progressively becoming more physical and aggressive. Our guys are working their asses off, hitting anyone who gets in their way. We can't afford a penalty right now, so I know I can't engage with Collins, but he's like a fucking gnat that won't leave me alone. He's known for being one of the biggest menaces in the league and lucky for me, I managed to get under his skin during the first period.

I'm back out on the ice, heading to their defensive zone for the face-off after they tried to ice the puck. I head to my position in the face-off when I see Eli Collins already there. He smirks and my jaw clenches. I cannot get in a fight. I cannot get a penalty.

"Fancy seeing you here again."

"Fuck off, Eli," I grumble, bending my knees as I crouch with my stick on the ice. "I don't have time for your shit right now."

"Maybe not," he quips with a bite in his tone. "I'd bet your sister does, though."

That's all it takes to set me off. Gone are the logical thoughts of not getting into a fight and not getting a penalty. This asshole doesn't get to say a single fucking word about my sister. Just as I'm about to grab the collar of his jersey, Lincoln punches Collins directly in the side of his face. His head whips to the side, blood instantly spilling from his busted lip, before he glances at Lincoln with a wild look in his eyes.

And then chaos ensues.

I shove Collins and one of his teammates knocks into my side, pushing me away from Eli. The last glimpse I have of him is Lincoln grabbing ahold of him. His teammate, Geralt, throws his gloves onto the ground and I follow suit as we square up on the ice. I throw the first punch, pain erupting in my hand as my knuckles catch the underside of his visor. Geralt's head jerks backward, but he recovers quickly as he lands his fist right along the side of my jaw.

My teeth clash into my lip and I instantly taste blood on my tongue. My hand fists the top of his chest protector and I jerk it upward as I knock him under his chin. Geralt mutters something, but the adrenaline running through my body has my heart in overdrive, silencing the noise around us.

I'm about to hit him once more when the refs are suddenly pulling us apart, forcing their way between us to break the fight up. My chest heaves and shallow, rapid breaths escape me as I try to collect myself, barely managing to do so.

Carson pushes my gloves against my chest, giving me a gentle shove back toward the bench. "What the hell was that about?"

"He fucking asked for it," Lincoln chimes in, blood dripping from his busted cheek. "He shouldn't have said a word about Nova."

"He knew exactly what he was doing," I tell the two of them as I hastily wipe blood from my bottom lip. I glance down the benches to where Collins is moving to get off the ice. He looks at us, lifts his palm to his mouth, and blows Lincoln and me a kiss.

I lift my hand to shield the action of my other hand as I give him the middle finger.

"Nash and Linc, get the fuck off the ice immediately." Coach Landry doesn't yell at us, but his voice is loud and harsh enough to have the two of us moving. With less than five minutes remaining in the game and the four of us each getting a five-minute major for fighting, we don't even go to the penalty box. We head straight back to the dressing room.

And our team ends up getting shut out.

***

"Nova's going to be pissed," Lincoln mumbles, touching the cut on his cheek again as we walk up to the garage door. Nova's been trying some new recipes and insisted I stop by on my way home to pick up a container of food she has for me.

I glance at my best friend as we reach the front door. "Do you want me to come in and be a buffer?"

Lincoln gives me a shrug of indifference. "I don't know if she's going to be happy seeing you in a similar position."

"Good call," I say with a chuckle, motioning for him to head inside. "I'll just wait here."

He rolls his eyes, lets out a sigh, and pulls open the door to find Nova standing on the other side. Her eyes widen as she takes in his face before her gaze flashes to my busted lip.

"I caught the last period," she says, shaking her head as her nostrils flare. She narrows her eyes at Lincoln. "Wish I wouldn't have, though."

"We're both fine, supernova," Lincoln tells her, his voice soft as he reaches to cup the side of her face. His face inches closer to hers, his jaw moving as he says something quietly into her ear. Suddenly, I feel like I'm intruding and clear my throat as I take a step back.

Nova glances at me, lightly pushing Lincoln away as she steps into the doorway and hands me two containers of food. "Can you drop one of these off for Riley? I meant to take it to her earlier but then Posey was tired and I didn't end up—"

"Nova, yes, I'll stop by her house now," I tell her, cutting her off as I take both containers from her. Lincoln steps up beside her, wrapping his arm around her back as he pulls her flush against his side. I'm glad my sister found someone, especially someone who's perfect for her like Lincoln, but it's a bit nauseating when they get like this. "I'll talk to you guys tomorrow."

"Thanks, Nash, you're the best!"

I give both of them a nod, backing away as Lincoln pulls her back into the house. I head out to my car and set the food down on the passenger seat as I head over to Riley's. It's already getting closer to midnight so I'm not even sure she's still awake. I hope she's already eaten dinner, but it's hard to tell with the way she gets busy and forgets.

The lights are on in her living room as I pull into her driveway and her front porch light flickers on just as I'm getting out of my car. The cold night air wraps itself around me, sliding through the material of my sweatshirt as I walk up to her house holding one of the containers of food. Grabbing my hood, I pull it up over my head to shield my damp hair from the breeze.

Riley pulls open the door as I step onto her porch. My gaze travels over her sweatpants and matching sweatshirt before meeting her eyes that are filled with surprise. "Hey. What are you doing here?"

A smile pulls on my lips and I tilt my head to the side. "Do you normally just open your door when someone pulls into your driveway?"

"If I know who it is, yes." She stares at me, narrowing her eyes for a moment. "I saw your car, Nash. I knew you weren't some random stranger."

My gaze is locked on hers and she challenges me

with her own. Riley isn't someone who likes to lose, so she doesn't dare to look away. A soft chuckle rumbles in my chest as I hand her the container. "Nova asked me to drop this off for you. Have you eaten yet?"

She gives me half a shrug. "I had a late lunch." She pauses, her gaze locking in on my bottom lip. "What happened?"

Instinctively, I lift my hand to my mouth, feeling the tender area that broke open earlier. "Hockey," I tell her with a tense smile. "You know how it goes."

Her eyes meet mine again and she lets out a soft sigh, her lips parting as she's about to say something. Whatever thought she has is cut off by her stomach rumbling. She glances at my car then back to me. "Do you want to come in and eat with me?"

The corners of my lips lift. "I'd love to."

***

"That was amazing."

I glance at Riley sitting across from me with a satiated and content smile on her face. Her eyes are gentle and warm and I revel in the way she's looking at me. There's a touch of exhaustion lingering behind her expression, but she attempts to cover a yawn, as if she's trying to hide it all from me.

"I am here to serve, Riley," I admit, half bowing as I rise to my feet and take both of our plates with me. "Your wish is forever my command."

"I can do the dishes," she interjects, rising from her

own seat. "It's the least I can do to repay the favor for bringing me dinner."

Shaking my head at her, I narrow my eyes in warning. "Riley, you don't have to repay me for anything, ever. I don't do things I don't want to do—well, that is if I have a choice," I add with a grin.

Riley looks annoyed for a split second before her expression dissolves and she shrugs with a smile. "I won't fight you on it."

"Yeah, you say that today."

Riley winks at me as she pushes away from the counter. The small gesture has my heart skipping a beat in my chest. I know her pregnancy hasn't been kind to her body, but God, she's glowing. She looks good pregnant, even if it is another man's baby.

"Why don't you put them in the dishwasher?" she suggests as she walks over to me. "I didn't even realize it was after midnight."

"As long as it doesn't involve you washing them, I'll do whatever you want me to do."

"That's a bold statement, Simmons," she says with a smirk, a glint in her eye. "Whatever I want?"

I stare back at her with a fire burning inside my chest as my heart stumbles over itself. *If only she fucking knew...* "Whatever you want, Riley."

Her nostrils flare and electricity sparks the air between us. Her lips part as if she's going to say something and a ragged breath escapes her instead. A pink tint creeps across her cheeks and she clears her throat, breaking the moment as she takes a step away. She laughs quietly. "I'll remember you said that."

"I hope you do," I tell her, my voice husky and filled with lust as I turn away to put the dishes in the dishwasher. Her gaze burns holes through me while I finish cleaning up. Riley's suddenly quiet and when I stand back upright and turn to face her, I notice her expression is different. Her forehead is creased and worry lingers in her gaze.

"How does this marriage thing work?"

"We can go to the courthouse whenever you'd like for a ceremony. We fill out the paperwork, someone witnesses the marriage, and then I can get the insurance handled."

She blinks. "That's it? That all seems relatively simple."

My heart constricts in my chest. It's too simple, really. "That's it," I repeat the words, nodding. "Whenever you're ready to do it, we can get it taken care of."

"Honestly, the sooner the better."

I don't ask her why because I don't need her to tell me. She's already been paying a lot out of pocket for her maternity care. She needs my insurance so she doesn't end up owing the hospital more than what she has in her savings account.

"I have to leave tomorrow night for the next week for a few away games." I pause, momentarily second-guessing the next sentence that falls from my lips. "We can do it before I leave if you want."

Her eyes widen. "Like, tomorrow morning?"

"You said the sooner the better."

Her throat bobs as she swallows. "I don't have a dress or anything."

Guilt floods me. Guilt because we're about to get married and it isn't the fucking wedding she deserves. I need a moment to remind myself this isn't real. None of this is real. It's a transaction—an agreement that helps to solve her current issues.

"You can wear whatever you're comfortable in."

Pain encapsulates her expression and the color drains from her cheeks. "Right," she says softly, forcing a smile onto her lips. "This isn't real."

"Right," I nod, the word a hushed sound that falls from my lips. "We don't have to."

"No, no," Riley interjects, shaking her head at me. "You're right. Tomorrow morning is probably best since you'll be leaving and I have some appointments coming up."

I force my feelings back into the box inside my chest and nod in agreement. "I'll come pick you up around ten, does that work for you?"

"That's perfect," she says with a smile, but it doesn't reach her eyes. "I'll walk you out."

We both fall silent and I follow Riley as she walks through the house to her front door. She pulls it open, stepping to the side to give me space to walk through. I cross the threshold, glancing over my shoulder to look at her.

"Good night, Nash," she says softly with emotion dancing in her irises.

I want to pluck each one from the swirling hues of green in her eyes. I want to dissect her emotions, I want to know her feelings. I want her to tell me everything she keeps locked away inside—everything she keeps inside that beautiful head of hers.

"Good night, Riley."

They are all things I'll never know…

Because I'm not entitled to a single piece of Riley Harris.

CHAPTER EIGHT
RILEY

I glance down at my hands and pick at the cuticle on my left pointer finger. Doubt rolls around in my mind, a stark contrast to the anticipation in the pit of my stomach. I don't know why I agreed to this. Actually—I do know why, but I can't help but feel like maybe it was a mistake. This situation is bizarre. When I was growing up and imagined myself getting married, this isn't how I pictured it at all.

"Are you okay?" Nash asks me to my left as he stops the car at a red light. We're only three blocks away from the courthouse and the emotional part of my brain is telling me that now is my chance to make my escape. Jump out of the car and make a run for it.

I glance over at him, fixing my face as I swallow roughly and nod. "I'm fine. Just feeling a little off this morning."

"What's going on? Did you call your doctor?"

Shit. I picked the wrong lie to tell him this morning. Grimacing, I shake my head at him. "I didn't mean physically. This is just… weird."

He instantly frowns before he looks back to the road and starts to drive again. "Yeah, I know. This doesn't have to change anything between us, Riley. It's just a piece of paper."

"You're right," I agree as the seriousness of the situation creeps deeper into my brain. Grabbing my smoothie from between us, I lift it to my lips, taking a sip. The nervousness grows within me as he pulls into the parking lot and finds a spot. I'm at the point where I'm beginning to ramble with no thought before I speak. "It doesn't mean anything. You're still free to date other people or do whatever it is that you want."

As soon as I say it, I want to take it back. I don't know why the hell I just mentioned that, but I did. And here we are.

Nash switches off the engine and slowly turns his head to look at me. "I appreciate your stamp of approval, but I'm not interested in dating anyone, Riley."

"You're not?" I move quickly, spilling the smoothie all over my white sweater dress. "Shit."

I need to learn to keep my damn mouth shut and watch what the hell I'm doing.

"I'm not looking to add any new people to my life," he admits as he glances down at the berry mess all over the front of my dress. "I think I might have a shirt in the back seat."

I stare at him for a moment, transfixed on the first sentence as I completely disregard the spilled smoothie. I don't need to ask him to elaborate. I don't need to travel down this road. It's my nerves and nothing more. It has nothing to do with the way my heart skips a beat when his eyes shine back at me. It has nothing to do with the way I'm hyperaware of every part of him when he's close to me. The way he smells, the way he laughs.

Goddammit, Riley.

"I can't wear one of your shirts, Nash."

"If you want to just wear that, I'm not going to judge you either."

I fight the urge to cry because goddammit, I'm tired of crying at everything all the time. "Fine. What do you have that I can wear?"

Nash turns in his seat, rummaging around in the back before he pulls out a blank paper bag. He reaches inside, pulling out a jersey before he hands it to me. "Here, you can wear this."

I lift it up, looking at the front and the back as I see it has Nash's last name on the back. "This is brand new. I can't wear this if you got it for someone else."

"Riley, just wear it. I bought it for Nonna and forgot to give it to her for Christmas."

"Okay."

He's silent for a moment as I pull the jersey on,

adjusting it around my stomach. "Are you ready?" Nash questions me, his voice tentative and quiet as his eyes scan my face. "I know this isn't an ideal situation, but you have to think about yourself and the baby."

"I know." I glance out at the front of the old brick building, my hand sliding over my stomach beneath Nash's jersey. *This is all for you, little man.* "Let's go."

Nash gets out of the car and makes it over to my side before I get the chance to get out myself. His hand is there, waiting for mine, and electricity slides up the length of my arm as I slide my palm against his. I don't need his help, but I let him anyway as I climb out of the car. Nash's hand lingers in mine and he shuts the door as he gives me a gentle squeeze.

I glance up at him and he gives me a soft smile that makes my heart flutter. My lips slowly lift and I swallow back my anxious feelings as I square my shoulders and nod. Nash's hand slips from mine as we start to walk toward the building.

The next half an hour feels like a whirlwind, like I'm lost as everything is moving around us. Nash and I walked up to the front desk and were promptly taken back. We didn't have to wait, which was probably best so I could stop overthinking everything. After filling out the paperwork and going over the entire process, we were ready for the ceremony.

"Did either of you bring anyone to be a witness? We need at least one other witness for the wedding," Mr.

Charles, the officiant, says as he glances at the door behind us.

Nash and I both look at each other. I didn't know we needed to bring someone with us. "No," Nash tells him, shaking his head. "I didn't realize we were supposed to have a witness."

The older man smiles at the two of us. "It's okay. People don't always know what the requirements are. Let me grab Cindy from the court clerk's office. She usually stands in as a witness for us."

"Thank you." I smile at the kind man as he disappears through the door behind the podium he was standing at. I turn to look at Nash who's standing beside me, except he's facing me. "This feels a lot easier than it should be."

He lets out a soft chuckle, his eyes shimmering beneath the harsh fluorescent lights above us. "Right? Anyone can just walk in here and get a marriage license. I knew it was a simple process and you didn't have to make an appointment, but this is kind of crazy."

"I will say, I do feel like I should have worn something a little nicer."

Nash takes a step closer, lifting his hand to fix the collar of my dress. "You're perfect exactly how you are, Riley."

"Oh my goodness, aren't you two just so sweet!"

I pull my gaze away from Nash, looking at the older woman who steps back in with Mr. Charles. She's a little shorter than him with curled gray hair that falls just along the tops of her shoulders. A smile lifts my lips and I try to ignore the blush that creeps across my cheeks as Nash drops his hand away from me.

"Nash and Riley, this is Cindy," Mr. Charles introduces us to her. "She's just going to stand here quietly as our witness, right?" he questions her as he gives her a sideways glance.

She lifts her hand to cover her mouth as she smiles and nods. "Right. I'm just here to witness."

Mr. Charles steps closer to us. "If the two of you want to face one another and hold hands, we'll begin." He pauses, glancing between us. "Do you have rings?"

Nash shakes his head, forcing a smirk that I know isn't fake. "This was an in-the-moment decision so we came a little unprepared."

"With a baby on the way, I don't blame either of you for not waiting," Cindy chimes in, winking at me before Mr. Charles scolds her with his eyes. If only she knew this wedding isn't real and the baby isn't his.

"Yes, we figured we might as well do it before the baby comes."

Why the hell did I say that?

Nash raises an eyebrow at me, but he doesn't say anything as he reaches for my hands and holds them within his.

"We'll start with you, Mr. Simmons. I'll read you the vows and you repeat them to Miss Harris."

I watch the Adam's apple in his throat bob as he nods. Mr. Charles begins to speak, but I don't hear the words he's saying. Fear flows through me, swirling in my stomach with the nervousness that has been building all day. Nash's thumbs rub the backs of my hands, his eyes soft yet probing as he silently tells me it's okay.

And then his lips move and his voice penetrates my eardrums.

"I, Nash Simmons, take you, Riley Harris, to be my wedded wife, to have and to hold, for better, for worse, for richer, for poorer, to love and to cherish." He pauses, his eyes burning holes directly through mine as his voice drops in volume. "Until death do us part."

My heart crawls into my throat.

"Your turn, Riley," Mr. Charles tells me quietly before he begins to recite the same lines to me. My heart pounds erratically, my chest constricting as I suck in a shallow breath. My tongue darts out to wet my lips and I speak the words to Nash, my eyes focused only on his.

"I, Riley Harris, take you, Nash Simmons, to be my wedded husband, to have and to hold, for better, for worse, for richer, for poorer, to love and to cherish, from this day forward."

"I now pronounce you husband and wife," Mr. Charles says, the smile evident in his voice as he closes the book in his hands. "You may now kiss the bride."

My heart skips a beat, my eyes widen, and I don't breathe for a second. We have to kiss. How could I have forgotten that part? Nash stares back at me, his gaze soft and warm, gentle and tender as he takes a step closer to me. If we don't do it, it will look suspicious and we need to make this look convincing so we can walk out of here with our marriage certificate.

I drop my hands from Nash's, meeting him in the middle as we stand in front of the wedding officiant. His movements are slow. He brushes my hair away from my shoulder and both of his hands move to cup the sides of my face. I tilt my chin up, my neck craning as I look up at him.

"Is this okay?" he asks me, his voice barely a whisper as his eyes search mine.

I pull my bottom lip between my teeth, biting down as I nod. My hands find his biceps and I hold on to him, inching close enough that I can feel his warmth radiating from his body. "We're just playing the part."

"Right," he murmurs, his thumb brushing across my cheek as he drops his face down to mine. His breath fans across my face, smelling faintly of mint. "They have to think it's real."

His mouth claims mine, soft and slow as his lips move against my own. My breathing stops as my heart tumbles over itself. I half expect him to move away, but when he lingers, I move closer, my lips moving against his. Time is suspended and our surroundings vanish as he kisses me with a tenderness that has my body melting.

His lips melt into mine, his tongue sweeping along the seam of my mouth as I instantly part them. The kiss deepens, his tongue sliding against mine as his fingers grip the sides of my face. The air around us is electric and he kisses me sweetly. His lips move against mine and in an instant, they're gone.

Nash pulls away, leaving me breathless as he presses his forehead against mine. I struggle to get a grasp on what just happened.

"Congratulations!" Mr. Charles's voice is filled with excitement and the sound of clapping comes from Cindy who is standing off to the side of him.

His forehead moves from mine, his hands still cupping the sides of my face as he moves away, just enough to look at me. There's an intensity burning within the depths of his eyes, his expression filled with emotion that mixes with something similar to guilt or regret. I'm not quite sure what it is, but it leaves me feeling unsettled.

It was just supposed to be a kiss to seal the deal, to show them none of this was fake, but it didn't feel like that. It felt like he was determined to reach my soul. To search the depths of my heart for the answer he was looking for.

Yet, it was none of that. It was as real as this marriage.

He's just really fucking good at making something seem convincing.

CHAPTER NINE
NASH

"What's wrong with your finger?"

Sitting on the bench, I look up at Caleb as I rub my thumb over my naked ring finger. My eyebrows pull together and I let go of my finger. "Nothing."

"Did you get hit in the hand or something?"

I raise an eyebrow at him and force out the lie. "Yeah, the one guy's stick hit my hand during the third period." That's an easier explanation than telling him I married Riley yesterday morning, but we aren't actually married.

"Are you good?"

"Yeah, I'm fine," I tell him, needing to steer the topic away from my finger. "You had a great game tonight."

Caleb nods, which doesn't surprise me. He doesn't come across as cocky or anything like that, but he's no stranger to being confident in his ability to play exceptional hockey. "I don't know how many I have left, so I'm not wasting any of my time."

He's been playing longer than the rest of us and although he's only thirty-three, he's definitely on the tail end of his career. With a young daughter at home, I know it's only getting harder for him to be away like this, but I also know what it's like to build your entire life around this sport. In a way, it becomes your identity and not having it is a terrifying thought.

"What are you losers doing?" Carson, Caleb's brother, chimes in as he walks over to us. He's changed out of his gear, freshly showered, and dressed to leave the arena. "Are you coming down to eat or are we going somewhere else?"

"I'm going back to my room and ordering room service," Caleb tells the two of us as he tucks his hands in the front pockets of his jacket. We're supposed to go back to the hotel with the rest of the team, but Coach Landry is used to Caleb doing stuff like this. He likes to go back so he can talk to his daughter before she goes to bed. "Take care of your finger and I'll see you boys in the morning."

Carson's forehead creases as he scratches the back of his head. "What's wrong with your finger?"

I let out a sigh, rising to my feet as I give a swift shake of my head. "Nothing."

He stares at me for a moment, almost like he isn't sure whether or not to question me on it, but he lets it go and motions toward the door. "I'm fucking starving."

Lincoln waits for us by the door with Rowan, our goalie, and the four of us head downstairs to where they have food for all the players. We all get in line to go through the gourmet buffet before we end up finding a table to sit at. When we're at home, it's hit or miss whether or not everyone eats, so I'm not surprised when there aren't many other guys from the other team downstairs.

Rowan asks Lincoln something about Posey and the two of them dive into a conversation as Lincoln gets to talk about one of his most favorite topics. He's completely obsessed with my niece and I honestly love it. He's the best fatherly figure Poe could have in her life. He loves her as if she were his own and really, she might as well be.

Carson inches closer to me. "Were you able to help Riley?"

I glance at him out of the corner of my eye as I carefully take a bite of my food. I don't give him an answer until after I chew, swallow my food, and make sure Lincoln isn't listening to either of us. "I was."

"And you were afraid she was going to say no."

"I was afraid she wasn't going to accept my help," I correct him, lifting my sports drink to take a sip before I turn to look at him. "She knew she was out of options and it was the best one."

"I'm glad," he says with a nod, a smile pulling his

lips. "I don't like the thought of her being in trouble or needing help with something. She's an exceptional woman and I've grown quite fond of her over the years."

His words instantly strike a nerve. My hand stills for a moment with my fork in my mouth before I pull the pasta from the tongs and slowly begin to chew as I narrow my eyes on him.

Lincoln glances at the two of us. "Fond of whom?"

My breath catches and I hold my shit together as I glance at him, attempting to appear unaffected. I hope to God he wasn't listening to any of our conversation before that.

"Riley," Carson tells him after swallowing a mouthful of food. "It blows my mind that her ex really fumbled her like that."

"I mean, he threw the entire idea of her and the baby out the window," Lincoln says, shaking his head as his jaw tightens. "Some of these men are real pieces of shit."

"I don't understand how you get someone pregnant and then just walk away," Rowan chirps, disappointment flooding his expression. "At least Nova has you," he tells Lincoln before he frowns. "Poor Riley has no one."

"Nova didn't always have Lincoln." All three heads turn to look at me and I shrug. "I'm just saying… Nova went through her pregnancy alone as well as the first two years of Posey's life."

Lincoln stares at me for a moment. "The thought of that kills me, honestly." His lips purse. "I know you're her brother and I wouldn't expect anything different from you, but you're the one she should truly be thankful for. You were there for her when she really had no one else."

"It's a shame Riley doesn't have family close by," Rowan muses as he finishes his dinner and looks between the three of us. "Maybe we all need to step in or something and help her out."

"Nash has been helping her a bit," Lincoln tells him before glancing at me.

"He has, hasn't he?" Carson smirks, raising his eyebrows at me, and I resist the urge to kick him under the table. Fucking asshole. He knows better than to go running his mouth about anything. I know he won't tell anyone my secret, but that doesn't mean he's not going to discreetly give me shit.

Coach Landry walks in, clapping his hands as he tells us all to wrap it up. I silently thank him, even though he doesn't know it. He just saved me from wherever the hell this conversation may have gone.

***

It's already late into the night when I finally crawl into bed. We have to fly out tomorrow morning to head to the next city and the thought of sleeping never sounded so good. Trips like this always have a way of taking it out of me. My body tends to get exhausted from the time changes on top of the grueling training and game schedule. Normally we get to where we need to be a few days early so we can acclimate but we were unable to before today's game.

As I lie in bed, I flip through the TV channels before settling on some baking competition. It's mindless background noise as I end up doom scrolling on my phone. I go through the various different social media apps until I end up watching a video about floral arrangements. Her voice sounds through the speaker, talking about a special arrangement they made for a wedding proposal.

The sound of her, the lilt of her laughter, has my heart constricting in my chest. Riley Harris has always been under my skin, but she's been progressively burrowing herself deeper over the years. The past six months have been a roller coaster with her life circumstances and after witnessing her vulnerability, I find myself with her constantly on my mind.

I open my messages and tap on her name, not hesitating to text her. I've been resisting the urge long enough and I'm tired of waiting. We won't be back in Aston for another eight days, and that's eight days too long.

NASH

Hey wife.

RILEY

Don't you dare...

NASH

Too late.

RILEY

I'll let it slide this one time.

NASH

I don't know, that might be my new name for you.

RILEY

Don't expect me to call you husband.

NASH

I would never.

RILEY

Good. How was the game tonight? I saw you guys won.

NASH

Can I just FaceTime you?

RILEY

Absolutely not. I'm naked in the bath right now.

NASH

So what you're saying is I have perfect timing.

RILEY

Nash Theodore Simmons.

NASH

Why must you do me dirty like that and use my middle name?

RILEY

Because someone has to get you under control.

NASH

You can control me anytime you want.

RILEY

Are you drunk right now?

NASH

I haven't even had a sip.

I half expect her to text me back but I'm pleasantly surprised when I see she decided to go ahead and FaceTime me. I slide my finger across the screen, answering her call as her face pops up in front of me. She holds it close enough that I can't see past her neck, but knowing she's naked right now has the blood rushing directly to my cock.

"Happy now?" she asks me, raising a perfectly arched eyebrow.

"I am," I smile at her, rolling onto my side as I hold my phone in front of my face. "How are you?"

She blows a breath out through her lips. "I'm okay. After you dropped me off yesterday, I ended up going into the shop and worked most of the day, and I definitely felt it today."

Worry floods me. "What do you mean you felt it? What's going on?"

"Calm down," she says, clicking her tongue. "I'm perfectly fine. I just get tired easily if I overdo it and I think I overdid it yesterday. I was just trying to keep myself busy instead of spiraling."

"If you're ever not feeling good, you'll let me know, right?"

Riley rolls her eyes. "I'm not going to bother you if you're hundreds of miles away, Nash. You have your own life and your own things to worry about."

"I worry about you. I don't like the thought of you being alone if something happens."

"Well, I don't like the thought of bothering you when you're not even home," she quips, narrowing her eyes at me through the screen. "If you're home and I don't feel right, I'll let you know. If not, I'll call Nova or something."

I purse my lips, mulling over her words before I give in. "If I'm not home, you can let me know after you call Nova."

"Deal," she nods in agreement. I hear the water beginning to drain from the bath and I know our conversation will be coming to an end so she can get ready for bed. "When will you be home, anyways?"

"A little over a week. It almost sounds like you miss me or something."

A smile breaks out across her perfect lips and the sound of her laughter fills my ears. "In your dreams, Simmons."

She'll be in them tonight… just like every other night.

"When I get home, be prepared to be sick of me," I tell her as I roll onto my back in bed, holding the phone above my face. "I wasn't kidding when I said I don't like the thought of you being alone in case something happens."

Her eyes shimmer beneath the soft lights in her bathroom. "And what are you going to do? You can't spend every waking moment with me."

"Maybe not, but I'll spend as many as I can."

CHAPTER TEN
RILEY

A fter spending a few hours at the flower shop, I left the rest of the work and closing up to Bethany. She started working for me right before I found out I was pregnant, and I've been relying on her a lot these past two months. I honestly don't know where I would be without her. She's helped me immensely to keep the shop up and running and she's going to handle everything for me after the baby comes.

As I pull into my driveway, I notice a sleek Mercedes Coupé parked on the street out front of my house. My eyebrows pull together as I don't recognize the car. I'm on high alert as I climb out of my car, my eyes glancing back and forth between my house and the unfamiliar vehicle. Just as I'm about to turn to head inside, I see an older woman climbing out of the front seat.

My anxiety lessens as soon as I realize that it's Nonna Rosa, but I'm equally confused about what she's doing at my house. For being in her late sixties, she looks exceptional for her age. Her days on the pickleball court keep her in impeccable shape. Relaxing my expression, my lips lift upward as I abandon my trek to the side door and walk around the front to meet her by my front porch.

"Hey, Nonna. What are you doing here?"

Her eyebrows pull together and she adjusts the weird-shaped bag on her shoulder. "Nash didn't tell you?"

Now I'm the one whose eyebrows are scrunched together. "Tell me what?"

Nonna waves her hand, motioning toward the front of the house. "Never mind. I thought I would stop by and bring you dinner."

"Did Nash put you up to this?"

She simply smiles, but she doesn't confirm if he did or didn't. "Let's get you out of this frigid air, honey. Come on," she says as she starts to walk up to the front door, leading me to my own house. A smile drifts across my own lips and I shake my head, laughing softly as I follow after her.

Nonna stands off to the side as she waits for me to unlock the door and she holds it open as I step inside first. She follows behind me, following suit as we both shrug off our winter coats and kick off our shoes. She waits for me to lead the way before she follows me into the kitchen.

"How was your day?" she asks me as she walks up to the counter and sets her bag down.

"It was good," I tell her as I go over to wash my hands at the sink. She pulls out a few glass dishes with already prepared food inside. "How was yours?"

As I attempt to reach for a dish, she swats at my hand. "You sit down and let me handle all this."

"Yes, ma'am," I say with a smile, knowing better than to argue with her. If there's one thing I know about Nonna Rosa, it's that what she says goes. And right now, this kitchen doesn't belong to me.

Nonna starts to tell me about her day as she busies herself, pouring herself a glass of wine before heating up the homemade lasagna and dish of vegetables she had prepared. My stomach grumbles in anticipation and I didn't realize how hungry I was until right now. I ate lunch and snacked throughout the day. Remembering to do so seemed to help my overall physical feelings.

I think my stomach just knows that if it's a meal prepared by Nonna, it's going to be the best damn thing it gets all day. Nonna walks over to the counter where I'm sitting and sets a plate in front of me, the aroma of the sauce and cheese drifting to my nostrils. My eyelids instinctively flutter shut and I inhale deeply, savoring the smell.

"Mmm, your lasagna is probably my favorite thing ever."

Nonna smiles at me as she grabs her own plate and

walks around the counter to sit next to me. "A little bird may have told me."

I raise an eyebrow at her as I cut a piece and slide my fork through the layers of pasta, sauce, and cheese. "Does this little bird talk a lot?"

"It depends on the topic," she says with a wink as she takes a sip of her wine. "You're a topic that's always been hot, although as of late, you seem to be on fire."

My heart flutters in my chest as the butterflies spring to life in my stomach. "I'm not sure what you mean."

She turns her head to look at me, her blue eyes twinkling beneath the lights in the kitchen as she stares at me. "I think you do."

"I've always been a topic?"

"Oh, honey." She lets out a soft laugh, shaking her head. "That boy has always talked about you. Lately he seems to be quite worried about you. He called me this morning and I told him I would bring dinner and stop by to check on you."

There's a part of me that is annoyed at the thought of him feeling like he needs to have someone come and check in on me, but at the same time, I'm also flattered. It creates that warm, fuzzy feeling that tingles all the way down to your toes. In a way, the thought is like a soft embrace. He hasn't been bothering me to see how I am, but clearly he's been thinking about it.

"I appreciate you stopping by, Nonna. I really do." I pause, taking a sip of my water as I give her a soft smile. "Nash has been helping me out lately and I know he's been a little concerned, but everything is fine."

"Has your pregnancy been rough? He didn't tell me the specifics but I know from experience that pregnancies can really take a toll on you."

I don't have to tell her our secret, but I'm also not sure I want to tell her what is going on with me and my pregnancy. The last thing I want to do is have her worrying about me when she doesn't need to. Nonna is an extremely caring and attentive person. I don't want to scare her at all.

"I've just been getting tired really easily. I have to be careful and make sure I don't overdo things."

That answer seems to be enough to satisfy her, although I can see the unasked questions burning in her eyes. "If you ever need anything, I'm only a short drive away. I would personally love to help you with anything you might need. Believe it or not, retired life gets a little boring sometimes."

"But at Christmas you were talking like you really have been enjoying it."

"Oh, honey, trust me, I do." She laughs, her eyes crinkling along the sides. "If I don't keep myself busy, that's when I tend to get bored, and honestly, I think staying busy is what keeps me young. If I sit around for too long, what happens if it becomes hard for me to get up? A woman at my age has to do whatever she can to stay young and spry."

"Nonna, you're hardly that old. I think you're the one who keeps us all young."

She purses her lips, giving me a knowing look. "Not many people can say they were alive to see their great-grandchild be born, let alone getting to watch them grow up." She gives me a small smile, but there's a sadness to it. "Sometimes it feels like I've lived multiple lifetimes and too many of them have been without Lorenzo."

Lorenzo is her late husband who was taken too soon. He was Nonna's partner in crime and her best friend. It's been at least ten years since he passed away, but I still remember the way he used to look at her. That man looked at her as if she hung the sun in the sky.

"He's the one thing that makes me look forward to whatever comes after this life." Her eyes grow misty, yet wistful as she stares at me. "I'm not ready to go anytime soon, but it's comforting knowing that when my time is over here, he'll be waiting for me."

"I can't even imagine," I tell her, my own throat growing thick with emotion as I feel her sorrow seeping into my bones. "I'm sorry, Nonna."

"Don't be sorry, honey. It's all a part of life." She waves her hand at me and then reaches for mine, giving me a gentle squeeze. "Just promise me you'll do something for me."

"Of course," I tell her, nodding as I hold on to her hand.

"When you find the one who makes your heart sing,

hold on to him and don't let go." She pauses as she looks at me with her soft and kind eyes. "Life is such a precarious thing that we never truly know how much time we have with the ones we love. Hold on to him and let him love you, because there's something indescribable about loving someone while being loved."

I stare at her for a moment, my eyes bouncing back and forth between hers as I let her words sink into my soul. "What if I never find him?"

"I promise you will," she says softly, a smile finding her lips once more. "He's already there, Riley."

CHAPTER ELEVEN

NASH

"Nash, net! Net!"

I glance across the ice to where Carson's skating along the boards. A defenseman is coming directly at him and he quickly sends the puck to me. The pass is effortless and I receive it with the toe of my stick just as I'm nearing the net. The goalie gets into position. I move to the right and he shifts with me. He's not anticipating my movements and he drops down just as I quickly divert to the left and send the puck soaring into the net with a backhanded shot.

"Fuck yes!"

Carson crashes into me, his hand hitting the top of my helmet. "That's my fucking Nashy boy!"

The rest of my linemen rush over to me, everyone celebrating my goal before I head over to the bench and skate past the rest of the guys, my glove hitting each of theirs. I move to the door and let myself in as we change shifts.

Coach Landry gives me a nod, his face as straight as always, but I don't miss the way he holds back a smile. It was a nice goal, but at the end of the day, it doesn't matter how pretty the shot is. A goal is a goal and we need as many as we can to seal the deal. Hockey is way too fast and too competitive of a sport to get comfortable and complacent. That's when things always seem to shift and go downhill.

We finish out the rest of the period with a two-goal lead before heading back into the dressing room. We all find our spots and sit down on the benches. I untie my skates, letting my feet breathe before I start to do a few stretches. A few of the guys eat a quick snack as Caleb, our captain, starts to talk, along with our coaches.

They go over some plays, Caleb gives us all a pep talk, and it isn't long before we're all heading back out to the bench for the last period. Our first line heads out, the puck drops, and play begins again. Sitting on the bench, I lean against the boards, watching everything happening on the ice. The first shift ends and Carson and I head out right after one another.

I skate past Rowan and his face is all business as he watches the play moving back into the neutral zone. I follow along, staying on my side as the puck gets turned over and play heads back into our defensive zone. Our defensemen make their way closer to the net, giving Rowan the backup he needs. The puck moves along the boards, moving behind the net before it ends up heading in my direction.

My feet move and I head toward it, attempting to take possession of it, but their winger pushes me against the boards as we both fight for it. He digs, pushing me harder against the boards, trapping my stick so I have no way to efficiently win the battle. He regains possession and sends it back across the ice to one of their players.

I move into a defensive position and just as I'm inching closer to the net, the other player hits a slapshot, sending it zipping through the air and landing directly into my ankle bone. Pain erupts along the bone and it takes everything in me to not drop to the ice. My vision blurs and I struggle against the searing heat at the base of my leg, but I can't get out of position.

I can't get off the ice, not now when they're in our defensive zone. The adrenaline in my body kicks into overdrive and I push through the pain, although I have no idea what the fuck is actually going on around me. My legs move on autopilot and as soon as play moves back down the ice, I head to the bench, half limping.

"Are you good to keep playing?"

I look at the equipment manager, my ankle fucking throbbing as I attempt to put all my weight on that foot. "I don't fucking know. I need a minute."

"Get Simmons back there now!" Coach Landry barks from where he's standing.

The assistant equipment manager slides his arm

around my back to give me extra support as we head down the tunnel. He gets me into the doctors' room and both doctors step inside the space. It's a whirlwind of activity as they pull off my skate, along with my sock, to inspect the area. It's already starting to swell and my skin looks fucking angry.

The poking and prodding send my senses into a spiral of pain.

"We need to get X-rays. It may be broken and I don't think he should play until we know for sure."

I shake my head, gritting my teeth. "I can get through the rest of the period. It will be fine."

Hockey is a sport where you cannot afford to get hurt. There's always someone who is waiting to fill your position. It doesn't take much for a career to end. Injured players are liabilities and once you start getting injured, you start to become more prone to it happening.

"We can't let you go back out," Dr. Forge says with a stern look on his face.

"You could do more damage," Liam, one of the assistant coaches, adds, equally not pleased with the idea of me heading back to the game. "Get changed and we'll get you back to your room and someone will have you on the next flight home so we can get medical imaging done and see what happens next."

Liam helps me out of the room and we head back to the dressing room. I try to push him away and hobble over to my spot on the bench, dropping down in a rush.

He gives me a look, almost like he doesn't know what the hell he's supposed to do next. Ignoring him, I drop my face into my hands, feeling the anger and despair engulfing me all at once.

"Fuck!"

***

"What did the doctors say?" Lincoln asks me as he takes a sip of his water bottle and tilts his head to the side. "Do they think you'll be able to play?"

I shake my head at him. "I'm flying home tomorrow morning. They want me to get imaging done and they'll figure out what happens next."

"Shit. This isn't good," Carson chimes in, his lips pursing as his nostrils flare.

"It's not ideal, but it's for the best," Caleb says, nodding his head. Leave it to him to always be the levelheaded one who views things logically instead of emotionally. "The last thing we need is for you to be on the ice and fuck it up worse."

"Yeah, if that happens, then we're really fucked," Rowan says, nodding along with Caleb. "We can't afford to have you out even longer."

I let out an exasperated sigh, settling into the bed as I feel the pain medication swirling around in my brain. My lips part, my jaw expanding as a yawn takes over me. The pain is still lingering but the pills they gave me have definitely taken the edge off.

"I'll see if Nova can pick you up tomorrow," Lincoln

says, motioning to my leg. "You probably shouldn't be driving."

"I can drive with my left foot instead."

Caleb gives me a look that makes me reconsider. "So you can fuck that up even worse once you're home?" He looks at Lincoln. "Call your sister. If she can't, we'll figure something out."

"Jesus, you guys are ridiculous."

"Nah, we just love ya, bud." Carson smirks as he rubs the top of my head playfully. "Come on, guys, we should let him get some rest."

"If you need anything, you call one of us," Caleb tells me, his eyes burning holes into my face. "Is someone going to take you to the airport tomorrow?"

I give him a look. "Yes, mother. They have it all arranged."

"Good," he says with a nod before he motions for his brother and Rowan to follow him out of my room.

Lincoln is the last one left. "I'll text you when I hear from Nova."

"Thanks, man."

"Of course." He smiles and nods. "That's what family is for."

Lincoln leaves the room after the rest of the guys do, leaving me alone with my own fucking feelings. It's not something I particularly care for, but what else can I do? My feelings are pretty dull and numb right now, so I sink deeper into them as I scroll through the channels on the TV before settling on another show.

I'm not sure how much time has passed since the guys left, but my eyelids are progressively growing heavier. I feel them beginning to close just as my phone vibrates on the bed beside me. I glance at it, feeling the urge to ignore it, but decide against it and lift it up. Closing one eye, I force the other to focus before I'm able to look at it with both of my eyes.

I was expecting it to be Lincoln, but it's not him. My heart skips over itself, butterflies fluttering in my stomach when I see her name.

RILEY

Nash. Are you okay?

NASH

I'm okay. How are you feeling, mama?

RILEY

We're not talking about me. Why are you coming home early? What happened? I saw you leave the game early in the third period but I missed whatever happened.

A smile pulls on my lips as I read over what she said again.

NASH

You were watching?

RILEY

I always watch.

That's beside the point. Nova said it's your ankle.

NASH

Yeah, I took a clapper straight to my ankle. They're hoping it's not broken but won't know until they do imaging.

RILEY

What time does your flight get in? I'll pick you up at the airport.

NASH

You don't need to do that.

RILEY

Yes, I do.

NASH

Lincoln was going to see if Nova could.

RILEY

Nash, stop arguing with me and tell me what time.

NASH

11 a.m.

RILEY

Okay. I'll be waiting for you when you land.

I'm fighting against the drowsiness from my medicine that is trying to pull me into a deep slumber. My eyelids feel like there's a ton of bricks weighing them down, but goddammit, I want to talk to her.

NASH

I'm glad it's you who's picking me up.

RILEY

Are you?

NASH

I am.

I don't like not being able to see you or talk to you.

RILEY

You can always talk to me whenever you want.

NASH

Not in the way I want to.

She doesn't respond at first and there's instant regret on my end for sending that message. The meds have me feeling a little careless and a little bold.

RILEY

What do you mean?

NASH

You're my wife and I can't even talk to you like you are.

RILEY

You can always talk to me like your friend.

I sigh as I read over her message, feeling a bit defeated and annoyed at the reminder. That's what it always comes down to and I'm tired of it.

I'm tired of just being her friend…

CHAPTER TWELVE
RILEY

"You are literally the worst patient ever."

Nash narrows his eyes at me. "Have you had other patients before?"

I can't help myself as I snort and roll my eyes. "No, I have not, but you really do suck at letting people do things for you."

"Coming from you, I don't accept it. You're the same way."

I picked Nash up at the airport earlier today and drove him to the outpatient facility where he met with some of the medical staff who work with the team. They took him in for imaging and were able to determine that he didn't fracture his ankle—surprisingly. The bone is bruised and the tendon right near his ankle was injured, but intact.

"Okay, but this isn't about me right now," I remind him as I pull my car from the parking lot and head out onto the street. "The doctor said you're not supposed to bear weight for a few days. That does not mean you can go skate."

"I have to get back on the ice, Riley."

I cut my eyes at him. "You have to heal, Nash."

"Yeah, but he said I should be able to play within the next week or two," he argues with me, repeating what I already heard the doctor say. He has to talk with the team doctors to make sure, but the one he saw today said he would recommend waiting a month, but he knows how grueling this sport is and that he needs to get back out there.

His treatment can be modified to accommodate his need to be playing, but he won't be playing at all if he doesn't try to rest and heal it in the meantime.

"If you fucking listen to him."

Nash tilts his head to the side, looking a bit shocked but also amused. "Damn, okay." He glances out the window as I take the next turn then looks back at me. "Where are we going?"

"Back to my house." I glance at him and back at the road. "Someone has to keep an eye on you to make sure you listen to the doctors."

"You don't have to take care of me, Ry. You need to take care of yourself right now."

I give him a sideways glance. "I'm pregnant, Nash, not disabled."

"Well, I know that. What I'm saying is that you don't—"

Something inside me snaps. There are no other cars around and I quickly pull mine off the side of the road, putting it in park as I turn to look at him. "I need you to stop arguing with me. If you really don't want to stay with me, I will take you home, but I would feel much better knowing you're being taken care of and that someone is making sure you are doing what you need to heal."

He stares at me for a moment, his eyes searching mine. My throat constricts and I attempt to push the emotion back down. "Are you okay?"

"No, I'm not." The words come out in a rush and I shake my head at him. "I am okay. It's you that has me fucking worried. I know it's just your ankle but what happens when it's something more serious?" I let out a deep breath, knowing I'm getting worked up for no reason. "Sometimes, I just really wish you would have picked a different career."

The muscle in his jaw tightens, his throat bobbing as he swallows hard. I watch his face transform, a small crease forming between his brows as his eyes grow warmer. His lips part, a soft breath escaping him before he closes them again.

"I watch every game that I can and sometimes I really just hate it. It's scary to watch you get injured, to see you go off the ice and not return." I shake my head, my nostrils flaring as tears prick my eyes. Stupid pregnancy hormones. "Sometimes you get hit so hard by other people, I'm afraid of what it's doing to your body. I don't know if the hits or the fights are worse."

He stares at me for a moment before his voice drops lower, the sound vibrating directly through my heart. "As much as I'm trying to focus on all the things you've said, the only thing I can think about is the fact that you worry about me that much."

Suddenly, I feel extremely self-conscious, like I just exposed a lot more than I needed to. "You're one of my closest friends, so I think worrying is natural."

His nostrils flare, his jaw tightening as he gives me a nod. "You're right. You don't have to worry about me, Riley." He reaches over, grabbing my hand as he gives it a gentle squeeze. "I'll follow the doctor's orders and let my wife take care of me until I'm cleared to do things," he adds with a wink.

My breath hitches, my eyes widening as my heart skips a beat in my chest as I hear him say that word. I force a smirk onto my lips, my eyes relaxing. "That's what a good wife would do, right?" I ask him, the playfulness lingering in my tone.

"Only the best."

***

"This smells amazing, Ry. Seriously, who knew you could cook?"

Laughter spills from my lips and I give him the middle finger. "I may or may not have picked up a few things over the years."

"Well, I happen to be an avid watcher of all things Food Network, so if you ever need any pointers, I got you."

Shaking my head, I sit down on the couch, holding on to my plate as I shake with laughter. "Bullshit, Nash Simmons. We both know you don't cook."

"Okay, you're right," he laughs, smiling back at me as he pushes his fork through the rice, mixing it with the vegetables. "Do you want to watch a movie or anything? I know I've kind of just moved into your house for the near future, but I wasn't sure what your plans were for the evening."

"I like that," I tell him as I reach for the remote and head over to a streaming app to see what movies they have available. Nash falls silent as he digs into his food and I can't help but smile at the sight of him. He's comfortable on my couch with his foot propped up and an ice pack wrapped around his ankle. He looks like this is exactly where he belongs and I can't help but feel like maybe it is…

We ended up settling on a comedy movie and we both finished our dinner. Nash pauses it for me as I take our plates into the kitchen and load them in the dishwasher. When I come back into the living room, I find him in the same place, smiling as he waits for me to get settled on the couch once more.

I sit on the cushion next to him, careful not to sit too close. I don't want to encroach on his space, but with the way his leg is propped on one side, I have no choice but to sit like this on the other end.

Nash waits until I'm settled and covered with a blanket before he starts the movie again. It dives right into the part where the two main characters end up locked in a room together. Nash chuckles softly, the sound vibrating in his chest as it resonates against my eardrums. I start to laugh with him, the muscles contracting in my stomach when the baby moves, kicking the side of my belly with enough force to make it feel like my whole body moves.

"Ow! Jesus Christ."

Nash whips his head to the side. "What? Are you okay?" He moves his body, his face instantly wincing in pain. "Goddammit."

"No, I'm fine, don't move!" I stare at him, the panic and pain evident on his face. Laughter bubbles up my throat and it feels inappropriate considering his expression, but I can't help myself. "I didn't mean to scare you. Look at both of us."

"We're quite the pair, aren't we?" Nash smiles through his pain, readjusting as he laughs. "I know why I'm in pain, but why did you say 'ow?'"

I exhale a deep breath, my hand rubbing across my stomach as I feel him moving again. "Sometimes when he kicks, it catches me by surprise and it hurts."

Nash's eyes widen and he glances at my stomach, his expression filling with wonderment before he looks at me again. "Is he moving right now?"

"He is." I smile at him as I nod. "Do you want to feel?"

His throat bobs. "Can I?"

"Of course," I say, my voice soft as I reach for his hand and scoot closer. Nash twists his torso, extending his arm as I press his palm against my stomach. He warms my skin and my heart as he stares at my stomach, watching and waiting.

The baby moves again, his little foot hitting the exact spot where Nash's hand is. He inhales sharply, his eyes immediately flashing to mine. "Oh my god, I felt him." Worry crosses his expression. "That was him, right?"

"No, Nash, that was the alien I've been growing for the past thirty-five weeks." I let out a soft laugh, watching the smile break out across his face. "Yes, that's him."

"Can he hear me if I talk to him?"

My heart stumbles all over itself as he looks at me with hope dancing in his irises. I swallow back the emotion welling in my throat as I feel the warmth from his hand still pressed against my stomach. "They said he can."

Nash stares at me for a moment, his lips twitching as he begins to lower his face closer to my stomach. I watch him as his eyes scan my belly, his other hand coming to rest against me as he closes his eyes and brings his mouth closer.

"Hey, little bud." I can see his lips lift into a smile as the baby moves once more, and he looks at me before looking back at my stomach. "I know we haven't formally met, but it's me, Nash. Maybe you've heard my voice in the distance before. I just want you to know that you have the most amazing mom in the world. She's been working so hard to get things ready for you and none of us can wait to meet you—especially her."

I quickly wipe away the tears that fall from my eyes, making sure I do it before he catches me. The baby moves again and Nash chuckles softly.

"I know, I know. You're running out of space in there, but I'm going to have to ask you to wait a little bit longer. We're excited for you to come, but we're not ready just yet."

An anxious feeling builds in the pit of my stomach. "No, we do not need you to come yet," I add, smiling as Nash looks back up at me. His hands linger before he pulls them away and I instantly wish they were back on my belly. "I still have so much to do."

"Don't you worry about any of that. As soon as I'm cleared by the doctors, I plan on starting to check off the things left to do on the list."

My breath catches in my throat, emotion washing over me again. "Nash…"

"I want to do it, Riley," he says, his voice soft and pleading as he stares directly into my soul. "Please just let me help you."

I get lost in the swirling depths of blue in his irises. "Okay." I blink the tears away, rolling my lips between my teeth as I nod, feeling a smile tugging on my lips.

Nash's eyes shimmer as a ghost of a smile dances across his face.

"Okay."

CHAPTER THIRTEEN
NASH

I stare down at my foot, the feeling of the pressure of the pad against my ankle making it even more uncomfortable. My fingers slide along the sides of the boot, attempting to adjust it as I look back at Davison. "Can't I just try skating without this?"

He clicks his tongue and shakes his head at me. "You heard what the doctor said. If you want to be back in the game this soon, we have to do everything and anything we can to protect the bone."

"So, I just make sure I stay out of the way. If I don't get hit, I'll be fine."

He stares at me with an unamused expression. "Nash, you know it's not that simple."

An exaggerated sigh escapes me and I reach back down to adjust the pad again. It's supposed to keep the pressure off my ankle from my skate, but it still feels uncomfortable as hell. It's still pretty sore and the padding just feels fucking weird.

"Do you want to play or do you want to have to wait a month or more?"

"I want to play."

He nods, his jaw set as he gives me a stern look. "Then get over it and do what you have to do."

After two days of complete rest, the doctors had me doing some rehab with the physical therapists, although with it mainly just being the bone, there isn't much to do. I was cleared to skate again today, but ordered to go slow. No game play for at least another week, but they advised me to get back on my skates and start getting used to it. I'm no stranger to playing and skating through pain, so I'm not worried about it.

What I'm actually worried about is when I'll have to go back home.

Even though I'm able to bear weight again, Riley told me to stay until I was back to one hundred percent. She claimed she liked having company. It makes her evenings a little less lonely, and I'm not going to pass up the option of spending time with her.

One day this will all have to end and I'll have no choice but to go back home.

Just a little bit longer with her…

Rowan comes strolling into the room, smiling at me as he walks over and claps his hand on my shoulder. "How are you feelin', big boy?"

"Pretty good. Ready to get back on the ice." I shrug.

"Doctor said just light skating, but he never said I can't skate with a stick."

A shit-eating grin breaks out across Rowan's lips and he shakes his head at me as he lets out a soft chuckle. "Forever finding a loophole."

"Come on, Simmons," Liam, one of the assistant coaches, calls from the doorway as he motions with his head. I head out the door of the locker room with him and we walk through the training facility to the rink. My ankle feels as stable as expected right now, but I ignore the nagging pain that lingers along the bone.

I cannot afford to miss any more time than the minimum of what the doctors expect. Even that is too much time missed.

My blades hit the ice and I'm acutely aware of the padding pressing against the bone of my ankle as I begin to move about. It's annoying and I don't like the way it feels, but it offers additional support and protection that I wouldn't have if I wasn't using it.

It feels good to be back... even if I have to temporarily skate with some adjustments.

Now, I'm just ready to get back into the game.

***

Since Riley has only been working mornings at her flower shop, she's already home when I get to her house. I find her in the living room, a smile pulling on my lips as I see her curled up on the couch. Her hand is tucked underneath the side of her face, her knees curled up as far as they can with her pregnant stomach.

Her chest rises and falls with each shallow breath she takes.

I stand in the doorway, watching her for a moment, my heart swelling in my chest at the sight of her. She looks so peaceful, her features soft and relaxed as she drifts through her dreams. I know these past few months have been rough for her and I'm just glad to finally see that things are calming down.

It seems like the easier she takes things, the better her pregnancy is for her. She hasn't had any dizzy spells recently, at least not that she's told me about. I know she has an appointment this week, so she'll know more about how everything is going for her and the baby, but so far, it seems like things have been better than they were.

Grabbing a blanket from the basket near the couch, I drape it over her, making sure she's completely covered except for her face. She stirs a little bit, but thankfully she doesn't wake up. I duck out of the room, heading into the kitchen to make dinner. I pull my AirPods from my coat pocket as I take it off and hang it in the foyer before returning to her fridge.

Music plays against my eardrums as I lose myself in the act, moving around the room as I get everything prepared and start to cook. Riley's been on an enchilada kick lately and they may not be as good as the ones from the restaurant, but making her dinner is the least I can do in return for everything she's been doing for me. All I can do is hope this turns out to be edible.

Time passes and I'm lost in the moment, my torso moving back and forth to the music as I finish up everything and get to arranging it on a plate. I slowly turn around, my shoulders dipping as my head bobs, when I stop in my tracks.

Riley sits at the island, a smile dancing across her lips as she watches me. Heat creeps up my neck, but I ignore it as I move over to her, setting the plate down in front of her. Riley looks up at me, her eyes filled with amusement as I pull my AirPods from my ears and reach for my phone on the counter. I tap the screen until the music's playing directly from the speakers.

"Dance with me," I murmur, setting my phone down as I reach for her hand. She slides her palm against mine, letting me pull her to her feet. Her lips part, a soft breath escaping her as she stands in front of me.

Time is suspended, my breath catching in my throat as she closes the distance between us, lifting her arms to wrap them around the back of my neck. Her stomach presses against me and I pull her closer, her body shifting sideways enough that she's pressed against my chest. She drops her face against me as I wrap my arms around her back.

"I thought you don't like to dance," she says softly, her body warming mine.

A smile forms on my lips and I move my head to rest my chin on top of her head. I pause for a moment, breathing in the scent of her before pressing a soft kiss against her crown. "With you, I do."

A soft sound escapes her and we move together, swaying back and forth in circles around the kitchen. The music sounds in the background, but all I can hear is the sound of my heart as it pounds erratically in my chest. Feeling her this close brings back the memory of that night at the gala.

"Nash," she says softly, my name sounding like a plea on her lips as she pulls away and looks up at me. Her eyes bounce back and forth between mine with the sparks of a fire burning within her irises. "Can I ask you for a favor?"

"Anything," I breathe as I instinctively slide one hand up to cup the back of her head.

"Can you kiss me?" The request tumbles from her lips in a whisper. Her nostrils flare, her tongue darting out to wet her lips. It's almost as if she realizes what she's asked me and she's suddenly self-conscious of it. "I just—I don't know. This is a weird time for me and I need something to make me feel. Something to distract me from the fact that I'm really here doing this alone. If you don't want to, I understa—"

I silence her with my mouth, my lips instantly finding hers as I drop my face down to hers. Her lips are soft and she doesn't move at first, like she's surprised I'm actually kissing her.

That's the thing when it comes to Riley Harris.

I will do whatever she asks me to do.

Her lips move and she kisses me back. I breathe her in, my hand moving along the small of her back as I hold her close, kissing her deeper. Her lips part and she lets me in, her tongue tangling with mine. It's been months since I've kissed her, but my god, it's something I'd never forget.

Electricity sparks in the air surrounding us and my heart pounds strong and steady in my chest, the pace a little sped up as my stomach flutters. She's been under my skin for as long as I can remember, but she's worked her way into the crevices of my heart.

I kiss her slowly, tasting and teasing her with my tongue until she's breathless, moving against me. My cock grows in my pants and I know she can feel it pressing against her, but she doesn't move away.

We break apart, coming up for air after diving in deep together. Riley's eyelashes fan across the tops of her cheekbones before they flutter open, instantly finding my gaze. "Thank you," she breathes, her voice barely audible. "I'm sorry I asked you to do that."

Lifting my hand from the small of her back, I move it to cup the side of her face, my thumb stroking her chin. "Don't ever apologize for asking for something you want or need." My gaze drops down to her lips and back to her eyes. "What if I told you I wanted to do it again?"

A soft breath escapes her. "I wouldn't stop you."

My mouth drops back down to hers and I kiss her with a tenderness, a softness, that seeps into my soul.

My tongue slides along the seam of her lips and she parts them instantly, letting me in.

Our mouths melt together and I kiss her with an intensity that's sweet and slow, tender and torturous. I kiss her until there's no air left in either of our lungs. Until we're breaking apart, coming up for air once more. Riley's chest rises and falls in rapid succession, short and shallow ragged breaths escaping her as her bright eyes search mine.

"Can I tell you something, love?"

She pulls her bottom lip between her teeth, biting down as she nods. Her eyebrows lift, a hopefulness washing over her irises.

"You're not alone." I pause, my heart pounding harder in my chest. "I'm right here with you." I let out a soft breath, emotion washing over me as I get lost in the swirling hues of green in her eyes. "You'll never be alone."

CHAPTER FOURTEEN
RILEY

The hot water in the bathtub sloshes around my body as I submerge myself in the tub. I lower myself until my ass is against the bottom and I lie back against the cushion, tilting my head back as I rest it on the pillow part.

Nash had practice this morning and left a few minutes ago, but he insisted on drawing a bath for me when I told him I wanted to get one before leaving for the flower shop. A smile pulls on my lips as my mind swirls around the thought of him. He's always been a patient and kind man, but how attentive he is has my stomach flipping over itself.

I know I shouldn't have asked him to kiss me last night, but I couldn't help myself. He's been staying with me for two weeks now and having him this close is driving me insane. It has to be the pregnancy hormones that have been making me feel horny and lonely. I know it's a line I can't cross with Nash, but kissing never hurt anyone.

It was probably a terrible idea because if anything, it's left me wanting more. I need a release, but I can't ask him for that. I'd be lying if I said I wasn't attracted to Nash Simmons. I would be lying if I said I didn't have the biggest crush on him earlier in life.

But I also know it's something I can't pursue. I can't allow myself the pleasure of feeling him… but that doesn't mean I can't fantasize about it.

My hand slowly begins to creep down my body, my fingertips dancing across my skin as I make my way between my legs. My heart rate begins to pick up and my stomach does a somersault as I touch myself at the thought of Nash and the things he does to my body. I let my knees fall farther apart, a sigh escaping me as I tip my head back farther, letting my eyelids flutter shut.

The fantasy starts with the thought of Nash walking into the bathroom. His eyes find mine from across the room as he lifts his shirt and pulls it away from his body, dropping it onto the floor while he stalks closer. My eyes roam over the tattoos etched on the skin of his right arm. His hands drop down to his waistband, undoing his pants before pushing them down the length of his muscular thighs.

I've accidentally seen Nash naked during our early twenties and I made sure to look away before he noticed me staring at his dick. Something like that, you don't forget, though. The size of it hanging between his legs. Except this time, he's rock hard and it's throbbing as he nears closer to the tub.

"Hey, mama," he murmurs, his voice husky and filled with need. "You got room for me in there?"

Pulling my bottom lip between my teeth, I nod, shifting in the tub as the water sloshes and I pull my legs closer. Nash looks at me, a smirk pulling on his lips as he shakes his head and moves along the length of the tub. My eyes follow him, watching as he moves to the side behind me.

His hands are gentle against my shoulders as he pushes me away from the side, inching me forward. His feet push through the water, his legs following suit as he slides in behind me. He pulls my back flush against the front of his body, his cock pressing against my lower back.

"Fuck, Riley," he murmurs, his lips brushing against my ear. His arms wrap around me, his fingers brushing against my breasts as he groans. "Can I touch you?"

"Yes," I breathe, nodding my head as I push back against him, letting my knees fall apart. "Touch me, Nash."

His hands move to cup my breasts, the fullness of them spilling over the sides of his hands. He slowly begins to knead my flesh, moving his fingers to play with my nipples. A moan slips from my lips as I let my head fall back against his shoulder, my eyelids fluttering shut. His mouth drops down to my neck, his lips soft as they move against my skin, tasting and teasing.

One hand abandons my breast, beginning its descent down my body. His fingers move down my stomach, coming around the front of my abdomen before sliding between my legs. The tips of his fingers brush against my clit, sending an electrical current through my body as I move against him. I moan again, this time louder as he drags his tongue along the side of my throat while simultaneously pushing a finger into me.

He moves his hand, slowly pumping his finger in and out of me as he presses the palm of his hand against my clit. The friction and the movement have me planting my feet against the side of the tub, my hips involuntarily bucking as he adds another finger.

"That's my girl," he groans, his teeth nipping at the outer shell of my ear as he starts to pump his fingers faster, his palm grinding against my clit. "Your cunt is so tight around my fingers. You're gonna come for me, aren't you?"

"Yes, Nash," I moan, my face screwing up as he applies more pressure with his hand. His fingers hit the right spots inside and I can feel myself clenching around him as my orgasm approaches. Another moan slips from my lips and he plays me with his fingers like a skilled musician.

"Come for me, love," he murmurs. "Goddamn, I

can't wait to sink my cock deep inside of you. I can't wait to feel you come apart around my cock."

I cry out, my pussy tightening around his fingers as he pushes me over the edge. My breath catches in my throat, my orgasm tearing through my body like wildfire spreading along every single nerve.

And then a loud knock on the fucking door rips me from my fantasy.

Holy fucking shit.

My eyes fly open and I move my hand from between my legs, grabbing the sides of the bathtub as I sit up in a rush. "Nash?!" His name comes out in a rush, my voice strained and three octaves higher than normal. "I mean, yes," I croak out the word, my voice getting stuck in my throat. "What are you doing here?"

"I came back because I forgot my phone and I heard something and wasn't sure if you were okay or not." He pauses and the silence is deafening. "Do you need help? What's going on in there?"

"Nothing," I tell him in a rush, my voice sounding nervous and off-pitch. My face currently feels like it's on fire while my pussy is still tingling from my cut-short orgasm. "I mean, I'm taking a bath. I—um—my foot slipped off the side of the tub and I hit it on the faucet."

What a blatant lie that does not sound convincing at all.

Please kill me now.

There's another pregnant pause and I resist the urge

to sink beneath the surface of the water. "Um… okay," Nash says slowly, his voice laced with curiosity as it sounds from the other side of the door. "Are you sure you don't need any help?"

Funny you should ask. If you want to come help me finish that orgasm I was having while fantasizing about you, that would be lovely.

"No, I'm fine," I insist, the words coming out in a rush. I shake my head at myself as I lean forward to drain the water from the tub, but then I stop instead. "Did you get your phone?"

"I did," he tells me, his voice trailing off again. "I should probably get to practice before I'm late. I do have my phone now, so if you need anything, let me know."

"Thanks!" I instantly wince at how weird my voice sounds right now, but try to brush it off and sound normal. "I hope you have a great practice." I cringe again because I made my voice lower than normal and that just sounded equally unnatural.

"All right…" He falls silent again. "I'll see you when I get home—I mean, back here, to your home." He mutters something under his breath. "Okay, bye."

I hold my breath as I listen to his footsteps, hearing them grow distant before I hear the faint sound of the front door closing. My lungs deflate in an instant, my body relaxing as I sink back down into the water until it reaches my chin.

That was a humiliating experience I never want to

live through again. I don't think I was truly convincing and I know Nash knows something is up, but he doesn't know what was going on here. He doesn't know I was in the middle of a goddamn orgasm when he interrupted me.

And so help me God, he will never know.

CHAPTER FIFTEEN
NASH

Climbing out of bed, I walk over to my bag on the dresser and pull out a clean shirt and a pair of pants. I've been living out of a duffle bag since I've been staying with Riley—only going to my house to do my laundry and swap out dirty clothes for clean ones. When I wasn't able to put weight on my ankle, I was staying on the couch. After that, she moved me into her spare room across the hall from the nursery.

I open my door, stepping through the threshold just as Riley comes out of her room, completely dressed for the day. Normally she doesn't leave this early for the flower shop, so I'm a little surprised. As I pause in the doorway, lifting my arms to grab the top of the doorframe, a smile lifts my lips as I look at her. "Where are you off to already?"

"I have an appointment with my ob-gyn this morning. It wasn't supposed to be until closer to lunchtime, but they called as soon as the office opened and asked if I could reschedule."

"What time do you have to be there?"

Riley pulls her phone out of her back pocket, her finger pressing on the button on the side to unlock her screen. She looks back at me, a smile dancing across her perfect lips. "I have to be there in thirty-five minutes."

"Give me, like, ten and I'll drive you."

Her eyebrows scrunch together. "What? No," she says with a soft laugh as she shakes her head. "You don't have to do that, Nash."

I tilt my head to the side, dropping my arms. "Do you not want me to? I don't have to come in."

Her expression softens as her eyes slowly search mine. "You would come in if I wanted you to?"

"Of course I would," I admit without any hesitation. I went to some of Nova's appointments with her while she was pregnant with Posey because I didn't want her to be alone. The same goes for Riley… although the situation is vastly different.

I want to be a part of Riley's life more than I've ever wanted anything. Maybe even more than I wanted hockey.

"That would be nice," she says softly, a hopefulness consuming her expression. "Nova came to some of my early appointments, but other than that, it's just been me."

Moving away from the doorway, I step into the hall, entering her space as I lift my hand to cup the side of her face. "It doesn't have to be just you anymore. I'm here, Riley. I want to come with you, but only if you want me there."

She pulls her bottom lip between her teeth, biting down as emotion passes through her irises. "I want you there, Nash."

"That's my girl," I murmur, the pad of my thumb stroking her cheek. Riley inhales sharply, her eyes wide as they flash to mine. I watch hues of pink dancing across the tops of her cheeks and she bites back a grin and moves to walk past me.

I resist the urge to push her up against the wall and instead, I let her pass.

"I'll meet you downstairs," she calls over her shoulder as she makes a quick dash—or more like a waddle—to the stairs. I watch her until she disappears, a little confused by her quickly getting away, but also satisfied that I have that effect on her.

I head into the bathroom to get on with my morning routine and after brushing my teeth, I make my way down into the kitchen where I find her sitting at the island. She's reading a novel I've been seeing her carry around for the past week.

"Whatcha reading?"

Riley looks up at me, a blush drifting across her high cheekbones once more as she slides her bookmark between the pages and carefully closes it. "Just some silly little romance book."

I plant my hands on the counter and lean on them. "Is it spicy?"

"What do you know about spicy books?" she questions me, her eyes narrowing slightly.

I push away from the counter, shrugging as I walk over to the fridge and pull out a bottle of water. "I've heard they've been helping people figure out different things they like." I pause, giving her a look of indifference. "You know, different kinks and stuff."

Her eyes grow wide. "Who told you that?"

A chuckle escapes me as I twist off the cap and take a swig. "It's not a secret, Ry. A lot of people talk about it. Especially the guys on the team whose girls are into reading." I pause, my gaze roaming across her face before resting on her eyes once more. "Have they helped you figure out anything you might be into?"

She cocks her head, her eyebrows drawing inward. "I'm not answering that," she says in a rush as she gets up from her seat and pushes in the chair.

"Because you don't want me to know or because you're afraid what might happen if I know?"

She steps directly in front of me, challenging me head-on, and goddamn my cock twitches. "Maybe it's neither or maybe it's both." She winks, biting back a grin before she turns away and starts to walk toward the living room. She glances over her shoulder at me, waving for me to follow. "Let's go before we're late."

***

Standing to the side of the bed, I stare down at Riley,

watching the doctor squirt lube onto Riley's stomach. She lets out a soft laugh, glancing up at me with her smile reaching her eyes. Instinctively, I take another step closer, moving until the fronts of my thighs touch the table.

"Who did you bring along today?" the doctor asks Riley as she presses the receiver attached to a small device and begins to move it through the lube.

"This is Nash," she tells the doctor, looking at the middle-aged woman with her smile still wide. "He's been keeping me company and making sure I'm not overdoing things."

"And feeding her all the enchiladas money can buy," I add, winking at her as she glances at me.

Riley laughs again. "Yes, can't forget that."

"Well, you sound like quite the keeper," the doctor says as she glances at me and back at Riley's stomach. She moves the wand around until a loud whooshing sound begins to come through the speaker attached to the device. "There's the little guy. He was trying to hide from me."

My eyes widen, amazement and wonderment flooding me as I stare down at Riley's stomach. My gaze quickly flashes to hers. "Is that him?"

She nods, rolling her lips between her teeth before her tongue darts out to wet them. "That's him."

"Holy shit," I breathe, my hand instinctively finding hers. "This is wild."

"It's pretty amazing, isn't it?" The doctor looks up at

me, a smile on her face as she moves the wand around. "He sounds perfect, Riley."

I watch as she pulls the wand away and wipes the goo from Riley's stomach. The sound of his heartbeat is stamped in my mind, stored away in my brain for safekeeping. I can't believe it—I can't believe I got to hear him. Something about this moment makes things that much more real. In a few short months, he'll be gracing us all with his presence.

My hand doesn't leave Riley's as the doctor measures her stomach and gives her a once-over, making sure everything is good.

"You're measuring right on track and everything else seems to be good. Your swelling hasn't gotten any worse, so that's a good sign. We anticipate seeing a bit as you progress and although you started to swell early, whatever you're doing has helped it to even out for now."

"You can thank this guy." Riley grins as she squeezes my hand. "He's been my saving grace lately."

"Well, I'd suggest you keep him around," she replies with a wink. Something in her expression shifts and her face slides into a neutral one, giving nothing away. "Your blood pressure is still higher than your baseline, so I think I'd like to start you on medication for it as a precautionary measure. We want to keep you and the baby safe for the duration of your pregnancy." She pauses, her lips pursing for a second. "Although he would survive if he came now, our goal is to keep him in as long as we can."

"What could be causing her blood pressure to be higher?"

The doctor sits upright on her stool, her head tilting back to look at me. "The cause of hypertension is still a mystery. We know of risk factors, but Riley has none of them. Other than PoTS, she's completely healthy." She pauses, looking at Riley and back to me. "She's at risk of developing preeclampsia, which can be a life-threatening condition marked by high blood pressure. We're monitoring her closely so we can catch it early if that is the case."

What the hell?

Why hasn't Riley told me any of this? When she said her blood pressure has been a little higher, she didn't once clue me in on the severity of it. She didn't explain what could really happen.

"Did you know all of this?" I ask Riley, my eyes desperately searching hers.

She nods. "They explained it to me when they first noticed my blood pressure." She pauses, squeezing my hand again. "They've been great about monitoring everything."

I believe her, but at the same time, I want to know more. I want to know everything. What actually happens? What can happen? The good, the bad, and everything I need to be keeping an eye out for.

"What can I do to help keep her safe?"

The doctor smiles, but it doesn't reach her eyes. "Unfortunately, there's no way to prevent it from progressing. At this point, making sure she takes the medication I'm prescribing her and that she doesn't overdo it. I would also like you to start taking note of your blood pressure daily at home," she adds in to Riley.

"And the medication won't hurt the baby?"

"She wouldn't give me something that would harm him," Riley tells me, her voice soft.

I look directly at the doctor, waiting for an answer from her.

"It will not hurt him," she assures me, nodding with amusement in her eyes. "While we do prioritize the health of the mother, we will not put the baby at risk unless it is our last possible option."

Relief overwhelms me at the thought of the medication not harming him, but I don't like her last sentence. Actually, it just leaves me feeling conflicted, which has my stomach knotting itself. I like that they prioritize her and at the same time, don't like that the baby is secondary. It's quite conflicting. Without Riley, there is no baby and I would be lying if I said she hasn't become extremely important to me.

Her survival is vital… even if it puts the baby at risk.

"Are we good to go then?" Riley asks the doctor as she moves to sit up. I quickly release her hand, sliding my arm around her back to help her into a seated position.

The doctor looks back and forth between us as she bites back a grin. "Yep." She nods, standing up from her stool. "I want to see you back in two weeks." She looks directly at me. "I'm counting on you to take care of her."

"I will," I nod, promising her as Riley and I stand up together, "I promise I'll keep her safe." Her hand instantly finds mine and I glance down at her, my chest constricting.

I'll always take care of her and she'll always be safe with me…

They both will.

CHAPTER SIXTEEN
RILEY

NASH

I'll be there in fifteen minutes to pick you up.

I stare at my phone, shaking my head as I read over Nash's message again. After my appointment this morning, he came and dropped me off at his sister's house. He wouldn't tell me why—only that he needed me out of the house for a few hours.

"Hello? Is anyone home?!"

Nova glances over at the front door just as Nonna comes strolling into the house. Posey climbs off the couch and goes running for her, the older woman scooping her up in her arms as she gives her a hug.

"Hey, Nonna," Nova says with a smile as her grandmother walks into the living room carrying a bag and Posey. She smiles at the two of us, coming to sit next to me as she sets her bag on the coffee table. "I didn't know you were stopping by."

"I had some things for you and Poe and figured I would swing by since I was running errands this way." She glances at me, a smile brightening up her face. "How are you, Riley?"

"I'm good." I nod, smiling back at her. "Can't complain."

"Nash is coming to pick her up soon," Nova tells her grandmother, wagging her eyebrows at her. She looks at me, an apologetic smirk on her face, although her eyes don't say she's sorry at all. "He's gotten pretty comfortable at your house, huh?"

"Don't either of you start." I laugh, shaking my head as I shove away my real feelings. "Nash and I are just friends, you both know that."

"Honey, I hate to break it to you, but friends don't look at friends the way that man looks at you," Nonna tells me, a soft snort escaping her.

Nova nods, giving me a knowing look. "I know my brother, Ry. I've never seen him this way with anyone else."

"Never seen who what way?" Lincoln asks the three of us as he comes strolling into the room. He looks back and forth between Nonna and Nova before looking at me. "What did I miss?"

"You're home early," Nova says, a grin drifting across her lips as she rises to her feet to greet him. She steps up to him, her arms moving to link around the back of his neck as he grabs her waist. He leans down and she lifts up onto her tiptoes, their lips meeting in the middle.

I glance away, feeling like I'm suddenly being invasive. I glance at Nonna and she looks at me, half rolling her eyes with a knowing smirk as she turns her attention back to Posey. Nova and Lincoln break apart from one another and she gets swept away in him as she starts to ask him how his day was. Lincoln went golfing with some of the guys earlier today, but he didn't disclose whether or not Nash was with him.

I think if Nash was doing something as simple as golfing, he wouldn't have needed me to get out of the house since he wouldn't have been there anyway.

The back door opens and closes, the sound echoing through the kitchen before bouncing into the living room. I sit up on the couch, glancing behind me, feeling a wave of relief as I see Nash walking into the house. His eyes meet mine, his face lighting up as soon as he sees me. He changed his outfit and his hair looks damp, almost as if he just got out of the shower.

"Hey," I say softly as he walks up behind me, his hands landing on the back of the couch by my shoulders.

His eyes drop to my lips before his gaze collides with mine once more. "Hey." His voice is husky, his lips parting as he almost starts to inch his face closer to mine. "There's my wi—" He abruptly stops himself, straightening back up. My breath catches in my throat, my heart pounding erratically in my chest. "Are you ready to go?"

Swallowing roughly, I nod as I begin to climb up from the couch. Lincoln says something to Nash as I say bye to Nova and Nonna, giving both of them hugs before kissing the top of Poe's head. The four of them all say bye to us, and I let Nash lead the way as we walk out of the house and head to the car.

Nash stops by my side, opening the door for me, and waits until I'm in my seat before he closes it and walks over to his own side. I'm putting on my seat belt as he climbs in behind the wheel and turns on the engine.

"So, what's the secret you're keeping from me?"

Nash glances at me, a ghost of a smile dancing across his lips, but he doesn't fully turn to face me as he begins to back out of the driveway. "It's not really a secret, but more of a surprise." He pauses as he reaches the street, putting the car into drive as he looks at me. "If I tell you, it will ruin it."

"But if you don't tell me, doesn't that still make it a secret?"

He looks at me from the corner of his eye. "Do you like secrets, love?"

"Maybe," I admit, my voice quiet as I look at him then glance back out the window.

"Perhaps I'll tell you mine sometime," he says softly, one hand on the wheel as he rests the other on the gearshift. "But only if you tell me yours in exchange."

***

"After you," he says, opening the front door in a sweeping motion as he stands off to the side, letting me walk in first. "I'm not going to tell you what the surprise is. I'm just going to wait until you discover it yourself."

As I walk into the house, I glance at him over my shoulder, my eyes narrowing on his. "You're not going to even give me a hint?"

"If you look around, it's kind of hard to miss," Nash tells me with a smirk as he steps into the house and shuts the door behind him. He kicks off his shoes the same time I remove mine and he takes my jacket before motioning for me to move. "Go ahead, see if you can find it."

I blow out an exasperated breath before I start to walk around the first floor of the house. My eyebrows are pulled together, my eyes squinting as I look in each and every room, looking for something different or out of place. Nash simply follows me around, his face giving absolutely nothing away.

"It's not on this floor, is it?"

He shrugs with indifference. "You tell me."

Another huff escapes me, and Nash chuckles as I begin to walk up the stairs to the second floor. He's right behind me, following me up each step. I glance at the room he's been staying in, walking over to that one first as I push open the door. It looks exactly as it always does—his bed a mess like he just crawled out of it because he insists making it is a waste of time.

We walk out of his room and I push open my door, giving it a quick once-over without stepping into the room. Nothing looks any different. I turn around to look at him, glancing at the door for the nursery before looking back at him.

"Nash…"

Emotion consumes me, my throat constricting as I roll my lips between my teeth and swallow back the tears that threaten to flood my eyes.

"Open the door, Riley."

My footsteps are light as I walk over to the nursery, my hand instantly finding the doorknob. I slowly turn it, my heart still in my chest as I hold my breath. I push the door open, lifting my hands to cover my mouth as tears blur my vision. Nash's hand grazes against my lower back and he eases me into the room.

I step inside, wiping the tears from my cheeks as I look around, my eyes scanning the walls. I never told him the color I wanted to paint, but he's clearly been paying attention to the different pictures I've shown him for inspiration. The walls are painted a soft gray-blue color with the far side a darker blue as an accent wall.

"You painted the nursery for me."

"Do you like it?"

Emotion chokes me and I close the distance between us, my body crashing into his as I grab the sides of his face. I can't stop myself as I lift up onto my toes, my lips finding his in an instant. "Yes," I murmur against his lips, kissing him again. "I love it."

"Good," he breathes against my mouth before his lips begin to move with mine. I kiss him with the fire that's been building and multiplying deep inside of me since the moment he decided to step in. Really, that fire sparked years and years ago, but only recently has it begun to burn as deeply as it has.

My feelings for Nash started when we were younger and they always felt forbidden, like something I couldn't explore. Perhaps things are different now. Perhaps everything between us has changed. We've shifted into unknown territory. Friends don't kiss friends the way he kisses me.

His legs move against mine as he turns my body, walking me backward until my back collides with the wall in the hallway. "I wanted to do this when I saw you this morning," he murmurs against my lips as he lifts his hand to push the hair away from my face, stroking my jawline with his fingertips.

"Do what?" I ask him, my voice barely audible as I drop my hands down to his shoulders, fisting the material of his shirt as I hold on to him.

"Kiss you until you're gasping for air."

His lips move against my own, soft and gentle as he kisses me with an intensity that has warmth pooling in the pit of my stomach and my toes curling. He kisses me as if time ceases to exist—like it is ours for the taking. He's attentive and tender, his tongue sweeping across mine, tangling and dancing together as he pins me against the wall.

My hands dig into his shoulders, holding on to him as I tilt my head back, granting him further access. Our surroundings fade away and the only thing that matters is him. He's all I see, all I feel. Nash Simmons grounds me in more ways than one. He's like an anchor—strong and steady, keeping me from drifting out to sea.

He kisses me slowly as if he's trying to siphon my soul from my body. He doesn't have to ask and he doesn't have to try. I'll gladly give him every piece of me; whatever he wants, it's his.

Nash moves his lips from mine and my lungs scream for oxygen as my chest rises and falls in rapid succession. He pulls back, just enough to scan my face as he bites back a grin.

"Mission accomplished."

CHAPTER SEVENTEEN
NASH

"How's your ankle feeling?" Caleb asks me as he skates beside me at the end of practice. "Do you think you're ready to get back into the game tomorrow?"

It's been two weeks since my injury and even though I don't feel back to one hundred percent, I'm close enough. I've spent enough time rehabbing it and missing games. We're starting to get closer to playoffs and although we're currently the number one seed, that can easily change. We still have plenty of games before playoffs start and it's a hard position to maintain.

All it takes is some fucked-up games and not gaining points to set you back further.

"I'm ready," I tell him, nodding as we reach the bench. "It's still sore, but nothing I can't play through. It's definitely feeling better than it was."

"Good," Caleb says, his lips forming a straight line,

never giving anything away, as usual. His brother skates up, along with Rowan, as practice has finished. "We need you back on the ice."

"You're coming back tomorrow, right?" Carson chimes in as we all head off the ice and back to the locker room. Lincoln meets us there, dropping down onto the bench next to me.

"Yeah, I've been cleared to come back if I feel like my ankle can tolerate it."

"Well, try not to get hit again," Lincoln says matter-of-factly, like it's that fucking easy. He, of all people, should know things don't work that way. The game moves so damn fast, you never know what is going to end up happening.

"All right, boys." Coach Landry's loud voice echoes through the room as he steps into the doorway. "I will see each of you here tomorrow for our morning skate." He looks directly at me. "Don't be late."

He's referencing last week when I showed up late after running back to Riley's house for my phone. The morning she was in the tub. The morning where I'm pretty fucking certain I heard her moaning in the bath. She claimed she hit her foot, but if I was hearing correctly, it almost sounded like she said my name.

I shake away the memory, although it's one I can't seem to get rid of. I'm dying to know if my ears were betraying me or not. I'm dying to know what the hell she was actually doing in there. My cock twitches at the possibilities.

"Earth to Nash."

The room comes back into focus and I glance up at Ford who's standing directly in front of me. "What?"

He purses his lips but doesn't call me out on not paying attention. "Rowan and I were talking about going out tonight. Did you want to come too?"

I shake my head at the two of them as I think about Riley waiting for me at home. "I told Riley I would take her out to dinner tonight."

Ford raises an eyebrow at me. "Are you still staying with her?"

"Yeah," I admit, shrugging nonchalantly as I attempt to brush his curiosity off and rise to my feet. "I don't think she should be alone, especially with her getting closer to the end of her pregnancy. I like being there to help her if she needs anything."

"I can't help but wonder what all you're helping her with," Rowan muses out loud, a chuckle following his comment.

Caleb stalks over to the two of them, hitting both of them in the back of the head. "Leave Simmons alone and mind your own fucking business," he scolds them with a scowl. "You both need to grow up and find someone to occupy your time other than the women you both pick up from bars."

Carson cuts his eyes at his brother. "We're just giving him shit. None of it is harmful."

Rowan grabs Carson's arm, giving him a look that

says to not start with his brother. The two of them are either getting along or arguing about something.

It's been four years since Caleb lost his wife and as a single dad, he's solely been focused on his career and his little girl. He already lived through the sleeping around phase that Carson and Rowan are still stuck in. Caleb found a woman he loved, married her, had a baby with her, and then lost her all within a three-year period.

He values the time and the moments he has a little more than his younger brother.

"Sorry, Nash," Carson apologizes, giving me a small smile. "I'm glad Riley has you there to help her. Rowan and I didn't mean anything bad by it."

"Yeah, I was just kidding," Rowan adds in, shrugging as he glances around the room, but no one else saw Caleb snap at the two of them. "I know you're helping her with a lot… and maybe helping her with your dick too."

Caleb slaps him in the back of the head again and Carson bites back a laugh, shaking his head as he ducks away from his brother. "You guys are both assholes."

I can't help it as I laugh at both of them, giving them both the middle finger. "I'll see you losers in the morning. Try not to catch any STIs while you're out tonight."

"I make no promises, but I'll try!" Carson calls out to me as I head out of the locker room, leaving them behind.

Not long ago, I would have been right there with

them. I never brought home women the way the two of them do, but I was never opposed to a random hookup here and there. So much has changed in the past few months, and it's not something I would even consider now. The women from my past, they never meant anything anyway. They were all just a distraction to keep me from going after what my heart really desired.

And now that I finally have my chance, I will not fuck it up.

***

"How do you feel about delivery and a movie instead?"

I look over at Riley as she comes into the kitchen, stifling a yawn. "I want to do whatever you want to do."

"As much as I would love to go to dinner, staying on the couch in sweats sounds amazing."

Smiling, I pull my phone from my pocket. "Where did you have in mind?"

"Phở?" she suggests, raising an eyebrow. "The baby really wants some."

A string of laughter falls from my lips. "Oh, does he? Did he tell you that?"

Riley's face lights up as she nods and I swear to God, my heart practically falls out of my chest at the happiness radiating from her. "He did, actually."

"Phở it is," I tell her, pulling up a menu on my phone. I add what I want to the cart, along with what she always gets, before handing it to her to double-check. Her eyes scan the phone, something dancing in her irises as she nods and hands it back to me to finish the order.

Two hours later, we're both on the couch with empty Pho bowls on the table and rolling credits of the movie. We settled on a rom-com Lincoln told me about one day, and the highlight of my day was getting to listen to Riley laugh.

Riley turns to look at me, adjusting herself to a seated position as she lets out a yawn. "Thank you for tonight," she says with a smile as she moves her blanket around herself. She was lying on one side of the sectional while I was on the side that met it. So close, yet I was hesitant to touch her. Hesitant to scare her away. "I needed that."

"Always, Ry," I tell her, turning on the couch to face her. "Whatever you need, I'm always here."

Her lips turn downward and a touch of sadness lingers in her gaze. "What happens when you're not here?"

"What do you mean?"

She motions to my ankle. "Well, you were staying with me while you were healing. You're back to playing tomorrow, so I imagine you'll be going home?"

I stare at her for a moment, my eyes slowly searching hers, scanning her expression before resting on her gaze again. "Do you want me to stay?"

"I can't ask you to do that."

"You're not asking," I retort, swallowing hard over

the emotion and hope lodged in my throat. I don't want to go. I've grown used to spending my evenings with her—most nights falling asleep on the same couch as her. "Tell me to stay, Riley."

"Stay with me," she breathes, her voice barely above a whisper. "I don't want to be alone anymore."

Instinctively, I move closer to her, wrapping my arms around her body as I pull her against my chest. "I'm not going anywhere, Riley. I've always been right here."

She pulls back, just enough to look up at my face as she scans my eyes, her expression unreadable. "You have, haven't you?"

"I have," I confess, with so much meaning behind those two simple words. "I always will be."

Riley moves closer to me, wrapping her arms around me as she curls into my body. I don't know how long we stay like that until I hear her breathing grow soft and even as she drifts asleep against me. I relish the way she feels, in her warmth and familiarity.

And the way she's nestling herself deep inside my heart.

CHAPTER EIGHTEEN
RILEY

The cool air dances across my cheeks and I pull my jacket a little tighter around my body as we step up to the glass. Nonna looks over at me, a bright smile on her face, before glancing at Nova and Posey. Posey bounces up and down in Nova's arms, her little voice growing louder as she points to Lincoln by the bench.

Nova asked me if I wanted to come with her and Nonna tonight to watch the guys. I haven't been to a game recently and it's nice getting out of the house for some time with my best friend. Nonna is practically one of the girls, anyway.

"Here he comes!" Posey exclaims, jerking her arm in the direction of Lincoln. A smile lifts my lips as I watch Nova move closer to the glass, holding Posey up to face Lincoln as he skates over to us.

He presses his hand to the glass and then blows

both of them a kiss, his gaze lingering on Nova as he winks. Nonna stands to the side, watching the three of them with the most heartwarming look on her face. When she lost her daughter, Nova and Nash's mom, it was very hard on her.

Their father had become a shell of a man, but was trying to keep it together for their sake. Nonna made sure she was around as much as she could be, although I know deep down she was struggling with her own grief while trying to mourn her daughter. A parent never thinks of losing their child, regardless of age. One night, many years ago, I found Nonna sitting out back at the Simmonses' house, smoking a joint while she cried.

It was Nova's first birthday without her mother. Everyone tried to make the day as special as they could while still honoring her memory. Nova got through the day better than I expected her to. She and Nash both mourned in their own way. Nova spoke of her frequently, claiming talking about her kept her memory alive. Nash internalized everything, never letting anyone see him crumble.

And Nonna—dear Nonna. She held everything together for both of them, along with their father. She carried her own grief, along with everyone else's. It was the only time I ever saw her cry and to this day, no one else knows about it.

Everyone had disappeared into the house after the party and I went out back looking for my hair scrunchie

I had lost while we were playing games in the yard. I stepped around their shed, thinking maybe it was back there, when I found Nonna sitting in the grass, a lit joint burning between her fingers and tears streaming down her face.

That night I sat in the cool grass with her and listened to the stories of Nash and Nova's mom. I lived through Nonna's memories with her until we circled back to her grief and she sobbed against my shoulder.

I never did find my hair scrunchie.

Moving closer to the glass, I look out at the ice, my heart stumbling over itself as I see him skating along the blue line. His stick is in his left hand, positioned in front of his body as he pushes a puck along with him. He leaves the puck by one of the dots on the ice and moves his right hand onto his stick as he begins to skate around, warming up the muscles in his legs.

Lincoln moves away from the glass after mouthing something to Nova and he skates over to where Nash is. Nash's eyes roam over all of us, his eyes instantly finding mine from where he's standing. He says something to Lincoln, nodding at him before the entire team starts to go through some of their warm-up drills.

Posey bounces again in Nova's arms and Nonna offers to take her as she walks around me to the two of them. Posey goes to her without any protest and Nonna's face inches closer to her ear as they watch the players while Nonna talks to her.

"Poe's been asking to learn how to skate," Nova

says as she inches closer, her voice dropping low enough that Posey can't hear her. "Lincoln sent me a picture of skates he bought for her earlier." She looks at me and down to my stomach before her gaze meets mine. "It's in our nature to want to keep them safe. Sometimes it feels like it was easier when she was still in my stomach."

"I'm terrified for the baby to be out here, honestly," I admit, my voice quiet as I shake my head to myself. "The world is such a scary place and there are literally so many things that can be a danger."

"Lord, isn't that the truth?" Nova gives me a knowing look before she looks back out at the ice to her brother and Lincoln skating. "I don't know how my parents did it with him playing hockey, honestly. It's almost worse now with them being adults. The hits are harder and the injuries are rarely ever minor." She glances back at me again. "I don't know that I'll willingly sign my kid up for any of this shit."

"I mean, Poe is still really little. I feel like her learning to skate comes with the territory with Lincoln, plus having her uncle who also plays."

Nova purses her lips and nods. "This is true." She tilts her head to the side. "Just wait until they start influencing your little babe. They'll be wanting to get him or her on the ice as soon as they can hold their head up."

"Him," I tell her, a soft smile lifting my lips.

"What?!" She claps her hands over her mouth just as

Nash comes skating over to the glass. I turn to look at him, the same time Nova tries to wave him away. "Come back later. You're interrupting something important."

Nash's eyebrows pull together. "What's going on?" His voice is barely audible but I read his lips.

"I just told her the baby is a he."

Nova's head whips back and forth, looking between Nash and me. "Wait, you told him?"

"It accidentally came out the other day," I tell her with a simple shrug, attempting to brush away the fact that he knew a secret no one else knew about.

It definitely isn't the first one.

"Holy shit, this is more serious than I thought," Nova mumbles under her breath as she turns to Nonna and Posey.

I keep my gaze on Nash's through the glass as he scans my face, making sure I'm okay as he usually does. "Don't do anything stupid or get hurt again."

"I wasn't that bad of a patient," he argues, a smirk finding his lips.

"You most definitely were, so you'd better behave out there tonight."

Nash tilts his head to the side. "Are you going to be the one delivering my punishment if I don't?"

Oh my god.

Warmth swirls in the pit of my stomach and my mouth is instantly dry at the thought of it. My pregnancy hormones have my libido through the roof and the last thing I need is this man turning me on in the middle of the ice rink.

Suddenly it doesn't feel as cold as it did when we first got here.

Carson Ford calls Nash's name, waving him over to where the guys are by the bench. Nash looks at him then back to me as the flames in his eyes burn brighter. My tongue darts out to wet my lips and he winks at me before skating away.

Nova moves back to me, now with Posey in her arms again. "Let's head up to the suite." Her gaze travels out to the ice as the guys are heading into the tunnel before she looks back at me. "I'm not going to lie, I'm a little annoyed that my brother knew you were having a boy before I did, but I can get over that."

"Oh, honey, a boy?" Nonna wraps her arm around my back, pulling me close to her side. "You are just going to have the best time with a little boy. No one loves their mother quite like a little boy does."

"That's not true. Little girls love just as hard," Nova chimes in.

Nonna nods. "They do, but it's a different kind of love." Nonna smiles at Nova. "Just wait until your next one. I just know you'll get your mini Lincoln which will show you exactly what I mean."

Nova smiles at her, warmth radiating from her expression. "I honestly hope so." She glances at me as the three of us start to walk together. "Do you have any names picked out yet?"

I shake my head, pursing my lips as we duck out of the way of a cleaning cart rounding the corner. Nonna ushers me away from it and I fall back in step with Nova again. "I have a few I've been thinking about but I don't know yet."

"Does this mean we can make the baby shower boy-themed?"

"Might as well," I tell her with a shrug. Everything I put on my registry was neutral just in case and I left it afterward. The way I found out made it feel a little weird to just randomly announce it to everyone. "I'd rather explain it to everyone then instead of having to explain what happened over and over to multiple people."

I don't tell her that I planned on waiting until he was born to tell anyone.

"Sounds like a plan." She smiles at me, winking as we step into the elevator and make our way to the suite level. Posey wiggles to be let down and she takes Nonna's hand as we file out into the hall. Nova grabs my arm, pulling me closer for a moment. "I just want you to know, if there's anything going on between you and Nash, I fully support it."

My breath catches in my throat. "There isn't." The two words escape me in a rush and nervousness lingers in my tone.

"Oh, I know," she says with a knowing look in her eyes and a ghost of a smirk playing on her lips. "I'm just saying that if there ever were to be, Nash is the kind of guy who would never break your heart."

I choke out a laugh, shaking my head at her as we start to walk, following behind Nonna and Posey. "You do know he's broken a lot of hearts, right?"

"Well, duh, silly." She laughs softly as we reach the suite, holding the door open for me. "That's because none of them were you."

CHAPTER NINETEEN
NASH

As I walk down the hallway heading in the direction of the players' entrance, I see Riley standing off to the side as she waits for me. A smile dances across my lips and my heart pounds erratically in my chest at the sight of her. I'm surprised that Nova and Nonna aren't waiting with her, but I also know how stubborn and fiercely independent Riley Harris is.

"Hey you," I say softly, stepping up to her as my hand finds her waist. Instinctively, I press my lips against her temple.

Riley glances up at me, a wave of nervousness passing through her eyes as she takes a step away from me and quickly looks around to make sure no one sees us. "Anyone could see you, Nash."

"What if I told you I don't care?"

She tilts her head to the side, her eyes narrowing on

mine. "Well, I do. You live under a microscope. The last thing I need right now is to be caught up in the rumor mill with people speculating you're the father."

Her words catch me off guard and I'm a little thrown off by the coldness she's cloaked herself in. "Would that be such a bad thing?"

She closes her eyes, inhaling slowly as her hands find her stomach. "I'm sorry. I'm tired and my feet hurt and I shouldn't be taking it out on you." She pauses, her eyes opening as her gaze settles on mine. "I know your history, Nash. I don't need people getting the wrong idea about us."

What if it's the right idea?

The words linger on my tongue, but I don't dare to speak them. I don't love whatever this shift is between us. Riley is unusually frigid as she constructs a wall around herself. I've known her long enough to know that when she's afraid of something, she projects. She retreats and protects herself.

I want to know what has her suddenly scared, but now isn't the time or the place.

"I'm sorry," I tell her, motioning toward the door as we begin to walk down the hallway. I do feel regretful for doing it. "I didn't mean to make you feel uncomfortable in any way. I shouldn't have done that."

"No," she says quickly, shaking her head as I hold the door open for her, and she steps out into the cool air of the night. "I don't want you to feel bad. It's just…"

She lets out a breath as we walk to my car. "It's complicated."

The corners of my mouth twitch because goddammit if I don't feel the same way. "Isn't it always?"

Riley glances at me, but she doesn't respond as she gets into the car. I close her door for her and walk around to my side, climbing in behind the wheel. I'm not sure if I did anything wrong or what happened from when I saw her earlier today. Something scared her—something that has to do with me.

"Do you care if we stop by my house?" I ask her as I pull my car out onto the street. "I need to get some clean clothes."

"That's fine," she says quietly, turning her head to look at me with a smile. As we drive farther away from the arena and closer to my house, I find a safer topic. I ask her about the game and Nova and Nonna and watch her face light up as she talks about my family. She fits right in with them... Always has.

We fall into a comfortable conversation and it isn't long before we're pulling into my driveway. I park the car by the garage and hop out after turning off the engine. I stop by the trunk, getting my bag of dirty clothes out of the back and meet Riley by the back door. I hand her the keys and she slides it into the lock, turning the knob as she lets us in.

We both kick off our shoes and Riley walks into the kitchen as I head into the laundry room to throw them into the washer. As the drum starts to fill, Riley appears in the doorway. The light behind creates a halo effect around her and I momentarily find myself captivated by the way she looks.

"Are you coming back here later to put your clothes in the dryer?"

My brow furrows. "Huh?"

Riley points at the washing machine beside me. "Your clothes are going to get gross if you wash them and don't dry them right away."

"Oh," I say slowly, what she's saying registering in my mind as I pull myself from the depths of her eyes. "Well, yeah, I know that. I just didn't really think it through other than knowing I need to wash my clothes."

She stares at me for a moment, her eyes moving back and forth from my right to my left as she lets out a soft breath. "You can wash them at my house." She slowly inches closer to me, stepping into the laundry room until she's stopping directly in front of me. "I'm sorry for earlier after your game."

"For what?" I ask her, closing the last bit of distance between us. My hand reaches for the side of her face, brushing a stray lock of hair away before tucking it behind her ear. "You don't owe me any kind of apology, Ry. I get it."

Her throat bobs as she swallows, shaking her head at me. "I don't think you do get it," she argues, reaching for my torso as she brings her body flush against mine.

Her dark hair hangs down her back as she tilts her head up to look at me. "You scare the shit out of me, Nash. You always have."

"Why is that?"

"Because you're the one person who can hurt me the worst," she admits, her voice barely above a whisper. "You make me feel things no one has ever made me feel before. I'm pregnant by someone else, yet you're the one I keep thinking about." She lets out a quiet laugh, pulling my face closer to hers. "The only thing I should be worried about is myself and the baby, but fuck it. Fuck it all."

She takes me by surprise as she lifts up onto her tiptoes and her mouth crashes into mine.

I meet her without hesitation, my lips seeking hers with desperation and urgency. Her hands fist my shirt, attempting to pull me closer as I grip her. I need to feel her closer. I need to just fucking feel her. My hands drop down to her waist and she breaks away as I move to lift her.

"What are you doing?" she says in a rush, her eyes searching mine with concern and shock. "You can't lift me."

I immediately stop. "Am I hurting you? Should I not?"

Her eyebrows pull together and she shakes her head as embarrassment consumes her expression. "No. I'm too heavy. I don't want to hurt *you*."

I scoff, a groan rumbling in my throat as it turns into

a growl. "You are not too heavy, Riley," I grumble, bending my knees as I grip her waist and lift her into the air. Her eyes are glued to mine, her breath escaping her in a rush as I set her down on the dryer.

"I've gained more weight than I thought with the baby and with the swelling…"

I narrow my eyes on hers, not mad at her, but not happy with the way she's talking about herself. "Riley, I'm going to need you to stop." I push her knees apart, stepping in between her legs as I pull her to the edge of the dryer, so her pussy is flush against me. I slide my hand through her soft locks, gripping the back of her head as I tilt her chin upward. "You are fucking beautiful. There isn't a single fucking thing wrong with you and I never want to hear that negative self-talk again. Do you understand me?"

"Yes," she breathes, pulling her bottom lip between her teeth as she nods.

Instinctively, I lean forward, my mouth seeking hers as I grab her lip with my teeth, pulling it free from her own grip. "I'm the only one who gets to bite your lip, mama," I murmur against her lips.

"Do it again," she half moans, her hands fisting the material of my shirt by my shoulders.

A groan vibrates in my chest and I nip at her bottom lip, pulling it between my teeth as I bite down gently. My teeth dig into her flesh, leaving crescent shapes as I pull away. My tongue darts out and I run it over the marks I left on her.

If only she knew the mark she already left on me.

Suddenly, all thought, all hesitation, and every single fucking inhibition is gone. My hands roam across her body as my mouth crashes into her. What started out as gentle and tender quickly becomes rushed and urgent. She grinds against me, her nails biting my skin as she kisses me deeper. Our tongues are tangled together and her hands grab mine, pushing them beneath her shirt.

I don't hesitate as I push up the hem, feeling her soft, warm skin beneath my fingertips. As I move them farther up her torso, they brush against the underside of her bra. Riley moves against me and I slide my hands around her back, unhooking the clasp before I move back to the front of her body.

My hands slide over her breasts, cupping them as I run the pad of my thumbs over her erect nipples. Riley moans into my mouth and I swallow the sounds, storing them in my brain for a later date. My lips trail away from hers, along her jaw before I begin to move along the side of her neck. I pinch her nipples, rolling the tips between my fingers.

"Tell me what really happened the other day in the bathroom, Riley."

Her throat moves as she swallows hard. "I told you what happened."

"You told me a lie, love. Give me the truth and I'll give you exactly what you need."

"And what is it that you think I need?" she breathes

before inhaling sharply as I push her shirt up to her collarbones. My mouth inches closer to her breasts and I run my tongue over her nipple.

"You need someone to make you come."

Riley sucks in another breath just as I pull her nipple into my mouth. "I was thinking about you."

Her nipple leaves my mouth with a pop sound as I lift my head to meet her heated gaze. "Thinking about me in what way?"

"In this way." She pauses, letting out a soft sigh. "My hormones have been crazy and I was imagining you in the bath with me."

My tongue darts out to wet my lips. "In your fantasy, did I make you come?"

"Yes."

Goddamn, she's so fucking sexy, and my cock is so fucking hard.

"I want to play it out in real life."

"But we're not in the bath," she points out before glancing at the washer. It's currently running with no clothes inside. "And I think you're washing water."

"Fuck the wash," I tell her, not giving a single fuck about it. All I care about right now is making her feel good. I mean, fuck… her legs are spread and she's sitting on my dryer with her shirt pushed up above her tits. "We can improvise, but I want you to tell me what you want me to do."

Her throat bobs as she swallows hard, but my girl never backs down from a challenge.

"Take off my pants and panties," she demands as she lets go of my shoulders, guiding my hands down to her hips. I hook my fingers beneath her waistband and she lifts her ass as I slide her pants and underwear down her legs, pulling them away from her feet. "I want you to make me come."

She could tell me to get down on my hands and knees and lick the fucking floor and I would.

She's naked from the waist down and goddamn, she's breathtaking.

"Fuck, look at you," I murmur, my hands stroking the insides of her bare thighs. "I want to devour you."

Riley clicks her tongue and shakes her head. "In my fantasy, you made me come with your fingers."

"But it would be so much better if you let me fuck you with my tongue," I retort, inching my way closer to her cunt. She's already soaked.

"Be a good boy and show me how well you can listen to what I tell you to do and maybe I'll let you taste me."

A rush of warmth goes straight to my cock and my balls instinctively constrict. If she keeps talking like that, I'm going to end up coming in my pants. Her confidence and her dominance are such goddamn turn-ons right now.

"I'll be a good boy," I breathe, my fingers drifting over her center. Abruptly, I stop and pull her off the dryer, holding her in my arms. "Don't fight me, Ry. I'm taking you somewhere else."

Riley doesn't protest as I carry her through the house. I can tell she's about to when I reach the bottom of the stairs, but I don't give her the option as I carry her up to my room. My room used to be the entire basement but after Lincoln and Nova moved out, I relocated to the second floor.

I walk into my bedroom, stopping when I reach the bed. I lower Riley onto the edge so she's facing away from the headboard. She looks up at me, her eyes heated as she watches me walk around her, climbing onto the bed behind her.

"I know this isn't the bathtub, but is this how we were positioned in your fantasy?"

Riley looks at me through the mirror that's positioned on the wall in front of us. "It is."

"I want you to watch yourself as I make you come. I want you to see what I see when I look at you. Nothing but pure fucking beauty, Riley."

Grabbing her knees, I spread her legs, planting each of her feet on either side of my thighs. Her pink, wet cunt is on full display in the mirror and holy fuck. There's already a damp spot on my pants from pre-cum.

I reach around in front of her, my hand moving down to her pussy as I push a finger through her lips. "This is your fantasy, babe. Tell me what to do."

"Slide one finger into me and press your palm against my clit."

I do exactly as she says, moaning as I plunge my

finger deep into her warmth. A shallow, ragged breath escapes her as I slowly begin to move my finger in and out of her while grinding my palm against her clit.

"Yes, just like that," she breathes, her head falling back onto my shoulder. "Add another finger."

I follow her command, slipping another finger inside as I start to fuck her harder with my hand. She's tight, clenching around me already as I rub her with my palm. "Look in the mirror, Riley. Watch the way I play with your cunt and fuck you with my fingers."

Her eyes are hooded, her gaze on fire as she watches in the mirror. I can tell it's getting harder for her to focus as she's on the precipice of that release she's been craving. Her body tightens, her hips involuntarily bucking as her cunt sucks my fingers deeper into her. She's clenched around me, gripping me hard.

"Eyes on me as you come, love. I want to watch you fall apart."

She clenches around my fingers, her head tilting back as she cries out in ecstasy. "Oh my god, Nash." Her nails dig into my thighs as her orgasm tears through her body. She fights against the urge to shut her eyes, her chest heaving and her jaw falls slack as a series of moans escape her.

My body is on fire and I don't even care as the warmth spills into my veins, the tingling sensation spreading from my balls. My cock throbs and I feel the wetness growing in my pants as cum spurts from the head of my dick.

"Fuck, you look beautiful while you come," I murmur, my eyes getting lost in hers as I'm riding out the waves of ecstasy with her. "I can't wait to see how fucking gorgeous you look coming on my cock."

Riley's orgasm begins to subside and I slowly pull my fingers from her, holding her in my arms, stroking her hair as I stare at her through the mirror. Her lips part, a yawn escaping her as she nuzzles her head against my shoulder.

We stay like that for a few minutes before her body starts to grow heavier and her breathing starts to even out. She looks up at me as I move away from the bed. "Come sleep, my love," I murmur, motioning for her to move farther up the bed. "I'm going to change and get you some clothes."

"I need to brush my teeth."

I nod, walking over to my dresser for a pair of shorts and a shirt for her. As I walk back over to the bed, I see her gaze drop down to my pants.

Her eyes widen, a pink tint creeping across her cheeks "Did you—did you come?"

"This is what you do to me, Riley." A sheepish grin breaks out across my face. "Were you expecting something different?"

"I don't know what I was expecting," she says softly, her eyes finding mine as she rises to her feet to get dressed. "But I'm not complaining about any of this."

"Did I meet your expectations from your fantasy?"

Riley lets out a soft breath, a smile dancing across her lips. "You exceeded them."

"Good," I tell her, nodding as I grab my own fresh clothing. "Let's get cleaned up and get to bed." I look at her. "I want you in my bed tonight."

"I like the sound of that."

I like the sound of you.

CHAPTER TWENTY
RILEY

My stomach shifts, my hand instinctively moving over my swollen belly as I feel the baby moving inside again. The further along I get, the more limited his space is in there and honestly, I'm beginning to wonder if it's becoming uncomfortable for both of us now.

For the first time in months, things finally seem to have settled down. My blood pressure has stabilized with the medication and as long as I make sure I elevate my feet, it seems to help with the swelling. Overall, the doctors don't seem to be too concerned with the way everything is, but they continue to monitor me closely, just in case.

I'm honestly grateful. I've heard too many horror stories of providers not being attentive or paying close attention to their patients. Of women knowing something is wrong in their body, only to have a doctor tell them they don't know what they're talking about. And then when shit hits the fan and their lives hang in the balance, everyone starts to wonder how the hell the health care providers missed the signs.

Maybe I should stay off the internet, because reading some of these stories freaks me out. I'm fortunate enough to have an amazing team caring for me… and to have this man who I don't deserve, making this all really happen.

Nash Simmons may not be mine, and I don't deserve the kindness he has already extended. When he offered to marry me—at first, I wanted to tell him no. Who the hell gets married for something like what we did?

But now, looking back on it all, I know why people do it. It has alleviated so much stress in my life. I don't have to feel the financial strain of paying for my own medical care right now.

Life has been so much easier because of Nash. It feels weird without him here. This isn't the first time he's had to go on the road for a game since he's been staying with me, but this is the longest he's had to go. The other times have only been a few nights at a time. This time, he's gone for a little over a week as they're playing on the West Coast.

I wish I didn't miss him as much as I do right now. He confuses the hell out of me, muddling my thoughts and fucking up my feelings. There are so many things I want to ask him—to see if I'm not just imagining things—but I can't bring myself to do it. If only I could let myself get past the underlying fear I have. I don't think Nash would ever intentionally hurt me, but the thought of letting him in like that is terrifying.

Sure, we've had our heated moments, but it could always just stay like that too. If we keep things the way we have been, it's easier for there to be a clean break. At some point, our arrangement is going to come to an end.

I'll have this baby and be able to get my insurance sorted out and then there will be no need for this anymore. We won't have to be married and he won't need to stay with me. Nash will be free to get on with his life however he wants.

And then what? What's left for me?

I don't think anyone truly wants to be alone, but if that's what it comes down to, that's how things are meant to be.

Nash Simmons doesn't owe me a damn thing. He has no commitment to me.

But I'd be lying if I said I didn't wish he did.

My phone starts to ring from where it's sitting on the couch beside me and I pick it up, my smile growing wider when I see his name. He must have known I was thinking of him.

"Hello?"

"Riley," he says breathlessly, my name falling from his tongue in relief. "Fuck, I needed to hear your voice."

My heart crawls into my throat as I hear the seriousness in his tone. "Is everything okay?"

"Yeah, everything's fine," he admits, sounding tired. I glance at the time on my phone, realizing he hasn't even played yet today. He must have just woken up from his pre-game nap. "I've just gotten used to talking to you and seeing you every day. This is weird for me."

"If it makes you feel any better, it feels weird not having you here."

"That actually doesn't." He chuckles softly. "It just makes me want to come home so you don't have to be alone."

The thought is honestly appealing. I would love nothing more than to have him lounging on the couch with me, laughing at some stupid show. Watching him cook me dinner because he insists that I don't need to lift a finger while he's around. He's had all of us fooled for years thinking he wasn't good at it. Turns out, he can follow a recipe pretty well.

It's been a weird adjustment, but I also kind of like it. I like feeling like I'm cared for… even if it's temporary.

"Thankfully you'll be home soon enough."

He's silent.

"Are you there?"

"Sorry, yeah, I am," he says, his voice gruff and half

muffled for a second. "I was looking at flights for tonight."

My breath catches in my throat. "For what?"

"To come home to you."

My eyes widen and I slowly sit up straighter on the couch. "Nash, stop being ridiculous. You'll be home next week."

"Yeah, like, next Friday," he retorts in an annoyed tone. "It's Tuesday, Riley."

"You cannot fly home."

He's silent again. "I could for the night."

"You're going to stress me out." I let out an exasperated sigh, although the thought of him being home is extremely appealing. I'm almost positive it would be frowned upon with his team and contract.

"I'm sorry," he says in a rush, the apology hanging heavily in his tone. "I was reading that there are different breathing exercises to help relieve stress."

I'm the one who doesn't say a word now. My mind processes and reprocesses what he just said. "I didn't know you read."

"I normally don't but I saw a pregnancy book at the store the other day and thought maybe it would be helpful for me to learn some things about it and babies."

My heart pitter-patters in my chest and my throat constricts. This man who owes me nothing is reading about pregnancy and babies. This man who doesn't get involved with anyone yet has been staying at my house every night for the past few weeks.

He bought a damn pregnancy book.

"Are you there?"

I swallow back my emotions, willing the tears to leave my eyes at the sentiment behind it. "I am."

There's sudden commotion in the background and it no longer sounds like Nash is alone anymore. "Shit. The guys just came to see if I'm ready to go eat before the game."

"It's okay," I tell him, feeling a bit disappointed that he has to go and I'll be in bed by the time his game is over tonight. "Give them hell on the ice tonight."

"Oh, you know we aren't going to lose without a fight," he replies, the confidence oozing from his voice as he laughs softly.

"You'd better not get into a fight," I remind him, half scolding him as I chuckle with him. "I'll talk to you tomorrow."

"Okay," he says after a beat of silence. "Hey, Ry?"

"Yeah?"

"I kind of fucking miss you."

My heart climbs back into my throat. "I miss you too."

"Good night, mama," he says, his voice soft and warm.

I close my eyes to the sound of his voice, absorbing it. "Good night, Nash."

The call ends and as if the baby can feel my emotions, he kicks my left side.

"You know, maybe it doesn't have to just be the two of us, little man," I say softly as I stroke my stomach, a smile pulling on my lips at the thought of Nash. He really is the missing piece I didn't realize I needed.

Maybe this doesn't have to be a temporary thing.

Maybe he has room for the two of us in his future…

CHAPTER TWENTY-ONE

RILEY

"Nova asked me if I could run to the store to get some things for today." I look at Nash, raising an eyebrow at him. "Do you know why the hell she would need any of these things?"

I show the list Nova texted me and watch Nash's face as he reads over the message.

Nova: I need a can of water chestnuts, some red beets, boba, and cotija cheese.

"She needs all this for the baby shower?"

"I have no clue," I tell him, feeling a touch of confusion, but Nova wouldn't respond to any other messages I sent her. "She asked if I could come drop it all off at her house and then she'd give me a ride to the venue."

Nash moves about the kitchen, almost acting like he's avoiding looking at me as he pours a cup of coffee. "I don't know what to tell you, love. My sister's strange sometimes."

"Yeah, but I don't get it," I persist, reading over the list again. What the hell does she need a can of water chestnuts for? "I don't even know what stores I need to hit to get some of this stuff."

"Do you want me to come with you?" Nash offers, lifting his mug to his lips as he takes a sip of the black bitter liquid. "I could see if I could get out of the team-bonding thing."

I shake my head at him as I play over what he told me last night. They have some team-bonding activity today, so he planned on coming toward the end of the baby shower. "No, you can't miss it. I don't want you to get in any kind of trouble."

"Don't stress over the list Nova sent you," he tells me as he sets his mug down on the counter. "Just get what you can and I'll come get you from the shower later, okay?"

"Okay," I say, nodding as I take a deep breath. "I'll go to whatever stores I can, but if I can't find something, she's going to have to do without it."

Nash walks over to me, his hands cupping the side of my face as he presses his lips to my forehead. "Good," he says softly, pulling back to look at me.

"Speaking of weird things, you didn't happen to see any packages outside yesterday, did you?"

Nash tilts his head to the side, his lips pulling downward as his eyebrows scrunch together. "No. What packages were they?"

My nostrils flare and I let out a deep sigh. "All the

furniture for the baby's room. I got an email that said it was delivered and I forgot to check yesterday evening. When I looked this morning, there was nothing there."

Nash's face relaxes, but he looks annoyed. "Where did you order it from? I'll call them on my way to the arena and see if they know what's going on."

"I can do it," I tell him as he takes a step away from me, collecting his keys and phone from the counter. "I hope they can send a replacement or track down the packages."

"Give me their info, Riley. You don't need to worry about any of that today."

"Okay," I agree, a smile pulling on my lips as I open my phone and go through my emails. I find the one with the delivery info, take a screenshot, and send it to Nash. "I just sent it to you."

"Perfect," he says with a smile of satisfaction as he looks at me once more. He goes to move and stops himself, the anticipation hanging in the air between us. It almost looks like he's conflicted and then it abruptly washes away from his face as he steps closer to me.

His hand finds my chin, tilting my head back as his face drops down to mine. His lips swiftly meet my own, kissing me sweetly before he pulls away. "See you later, love."

My heart is in my throat and it takes me a second to get the word out. "Bye."

Contentment floods me as I watch Nash head out

the door. Just the fact that I know I'll see him later brings me the sense of peace I need.

He makes everything easier, while at the same time making everything complicated. My heart knows what it wants and it wants him.

***

Nova was expecting me when I got to her house and she didn't pay any attention to the bags of random shit I brought her from the store. She simply thanked me, put it on the counter, and ushered me out the door, claiming we were going to be late if we didn't leave immediately.

We were going to be late because of the wild-goose chase she sent me on, looking for a bunch of ingredients that aren't needed in one recipe.

When we pull up to the old historical mansion, the breath leaves my lungs in a rush. It's a beautiful manor built of stone with ivy sweeping up the sides of the building. I've heard of Greendale Estate before, but this is the first time I'm seeing it in person.

It's tucked down a long lane, surrounded by the most beautiful gardens. Nova walks with me as we make our way to the front door. The small parking lot is already filled with cars and when we walk inside, I'm blown away by the delicate flowers and pastel colors decorating the inside.

Nonna and Posey are in the foyer area, Posey running over to me to give my stomach a kiss before her small hand slips into mine and she pulls me with her. We walk into the main room and I see the familiar faces of all our friends and family.

Bethany waves at me from where she's fixing an arrangement on one of the tables. At the table next to her, I see Mia Landry, Nash's coach's daughter, Quinn, the team's physical therapist, and a few of the other players' wives and girlfriends.

At another table are some of Nash and Nova's family that I've known for many years, and at another are a few of my cousins and my mother. I'm surprised to see her and I walk right to her as she stands up and pulls me in for a hug.

"You are glowing, baby," my mother says as she cups the sides of my face. "How are you feeling?"

Even though she lives farther away, she's been checking in with me periodically throughout my pregnancy. It's not the same as having her nearby, but I got used to being separated from my family long ago. We've never had a close relationship and although it's something I wish we had, it's something I accepted years ago.

"I'm good. Everything is going pretty well now," I tell her, a smile on my lips. "Thank you for coming."

"You know I wouldn't have missed it."

The smile on my face feels a little more forced and I nod at her. It's such a lie and she's most likely here because of the guilt, but it's fine. This is how my mother operates. When I told her the news of being pregnant and that I wasn't with the father, she was less than thrilled. She came around to it and has been supportive since, but only from afar and only when it suits her.

Leaving my mother with my cousins, I turn around, spotting a table with a few faces I didn't expect to see. The Ford brothers, Rowan, Hayes, and Lincoln are all sitting together. A confused smile pulls on my lips as I walk over to the guys. Some of their significant others aren't here, but the guys weren't supposed to come from what Nova told me.

They were all supposed to be at a team-bonding activity.

"What are you guys doing here?"

They all take turns pulling me in for a hug, the last being Carson as he leaves his arm wrapped around me. "It was only for some of the guys," he tells me. "We all had different activities we were doing and we finished early. Nash should be here in a little bit."

Disappointment washes over me and what he says seems a little strange, but I don't question him on it. I don't fully know everything the team does together, so, in a way, it kind of makes sense. Although, it's a little weird that these five ended up together and Nash wasn't with any of them.

"Come on," Nova says, linking her arm through mine. "We need you at the front of the room." She turns to the entire room. "Food is in the kitchen if everyone wants to help themselves."

Nova leads me into the massive kitchen, ushering me along the line as I fill my plate with some food.

After I get everything I need, she takes me back into the main room, taking me toward the fireplace where there's a balloon arch over the small couch in the center. I take my seat and Nova leaves me to eat as she goes to find Posey.

Everyone files back into the room, taking their seats as they start to eat. I look around the room, watching everyone as they fall into their own comfortable conversations and suddenly, I feel completely alone in a room full of people. Sadness consumes me, my chest growing tighter as I set my fork down on my plate.

I don't want to burden anyone with my feelings or my thoughts, but goddamn, this is increasingly becoming uncomfortable. Nova is with Posey. Nonna is with the boys. Everyone is at their table, talking and laughing, and then there's me.

I swallow roughly, pushing back the emotion that threatens to consume me, no thanks to the pregnancy hormones, when I hear the front door quietly opening. Turning my head to look, I stare at the doorway, relief flooding me as he steps past the threshold. His eyes find mine in an instant, his face lighting up as soon as he sees me.

He doesn't stop to say anything to anyone. Instead, he walks directly to me, not stopping until he's standing directly in front of me. "Hey you," he murmurs, his words only meant for me. "Sorry I didn't get here sooner."

Solace sweeps across me. "It's okay." I smile up at

him, scooting over. Nash doesn't hesitate to sit down next to me, his arm instinctively resting on the top of the couch along my shoulders. "You're here now."

He hands me a small box.

"What's this?"

"I'm appalled that you expected me to show up empty-handed to your baby shower." He lifts his hand to his chest. "You wound me, Riley." Then he winks at me. "Open it."

My gaze drops down to the small box and I pull the ribbon before tearing the paper away. Our surroundings fade away and it's just the two of us as I lift the lid. A gasp escapes me, emotion building in my chest as I see the world's smallest Aston Archers jersey.

"Oh my god, look at this," I murmur, lifting it from the box as my eyes scan the front of the infant-sized jersey. I didn't even know they made ones this small. "This is so adorable."

"Flip it over," he says softly, his eyes gently probing mine.

My breath catches in my throat as I flip it over. Instead of a last name, it says BABY across the back of the jersey. My vision blurs as I see the number on the back.

17.

Nash's number.

"I wasn't sure if you decided on a name yet, so I figured 'baby' was the safest bet," he explains with a nervousness as a ghost of a smile plays across his lips.

"It's perfect," I tell him, my gaze burning directly into his soul as my heart swells inside my chest.

You're perfect.

***

"Riley, we're home."

My eyelids slowly lift and I move to sit up straighter in my seat as I look out the window. Nash parks the car in my driveway and kills the engine as he turns to look at me. "I didn't mean to fall asleep."

"It's okay," he says softly with the gentlest smile. "You had a long and exhausting day, so it's only natural to be tired. Let's get you inside so you can get comfortable."

"Thank you," I tell him, letting out a yawn. "I want to help carry some of the baby's things inside."

Nash narrows his eyes on me. "You can carry a shirt or a book. I get to decide what is or isn't too heavy for you."

A soft laugh slips from my lips and I roll my eyes at him. "Yes, sir."

"I like that." A heated look grows in his eyes. "Maybe I need to order you around more often."

"Yeah, because I'm not going to argue with you or anything," I say with sarcasm heavy in my tone.

A smirk drifts across his lips. "It turns me on even more when you do that shit."

A rush of warmth goes straight to my center and I quickly get out of the enclosed space before this ends up turning into something in the front seat of his car. I meet Nash at the back of the car and he hands me two gift bags that barely weigh anything. He instructs me to go open the door and I do as he says, unlocking the front door and holding it open for him as he carries in a few boxes.

He leaves them at the top of the stairs then heads back out to get another load. I head over to the nursery, letting myself into the baby's room. As I step inside, I stop in my tracks, the air leaving my lungs in a rush. Somehow the same crib, changing table, and dresser I ordered are all inside the nursery perfectly constructed and arranged.

I glance around the room, tears springing to my eyes as I take it all in. There's a rug by the crib and curtains hung by the windows. Everything I ordered and thought was missing is here.

His footsteps are light as he walks into the room, setting down a few boxes as I turn around to face him. Nash's eyes meet mine.

"Where did you get these things?" I question him, attempting to blink away the tears. "This is everything I ordered. Everything that was missing."

A smile lifts Nash's lips as his eyes probe mine. "They were never missing, Ry." A soft chuckle escapes him as he closes the distance between us. "I hid them yesterday afternoon."

"Is this where you were earlier today?"

His grin turns sheepish as he nods. "There was no

team building activity. I needed to get you out of the house to put everything together before you got home."

All of this—he did it all for me.

Nash lifts his hands to cup the sides of my face, his thumbs sweeping across my cheeks to catch the tears as they fall from my eyes.

"You gave me my dream nursery."

Emotion envelops his expression. "I just want you to be happy, Riley. You deserve all the good in the world."

"I am happy," I tell him, stepping closer to him as I lift my hands to his waist. Nash Simmons has the biggest heart. The sweetest soul. *He is the kindest man.* "You make me happy."

"Riley..." he murmurs, my name like a plea on his lips as a fire burns brightly in his eyes. He's waiting to make his play, but as I lift up onto my toes, I beat him to it.

CHAPTER TWENTY-TWO

NASH

Riley's lips are soft, yet urgent, tender, yet desperate as they move against mine. What starts out as slow and gentle quickly turns into something intense, something demanding. I match the shifting energy immediately, my mouth moving with hers, tongues tangling in a delicious dance. I could kiss her for the rest of my fucking life. She tastes like strawberries, and I'm instantly drunk from kissing her.

"I want you, Nash," she murmurs against my mouth, her lips dancing across my own. "I *need* you."

My head swims, my heart pounds, and she surrounds me. My cock springs to life in my pants, hot and throbbing as she presses herself against me, kissing me with a need that's been burning for a fucking lifetime.

Spinning her around, I back her out of the nursery and into the hallway. Riley's hands slide up to my chest and she takes over, pressing me against the wall as the kiss deepens. Her tongue slides against mine, one of her hands leaving my chest as she reaches for the doorknob beside her.

She manages to get it open, both of her hands moving back to the collar of my shirt as she drags me away from the wall, pulling me into her bedroom. My hands find her hips, spinning her around as I back her farther into the room, not stopping until the backs of her legs are hitting the edge of the bed.

We break apart, our breathing ragged as we struggle to catch our breaths. Riley's chest rises and falls in rapid succession as she reaches down to the hem of her shirt. My nostrils flare, a fire burning inside me as I watch her slowly lift it up and over her head before dropping it onto the floor.

My eyes scan over her body, traveling over her swollen stomach, landing on her full breasts as she unhooks her bra and tosses it with her shirt. Her nipples grow hard under my gaze and I resist the urge to go to her, to touch her and taste her. I'm waiting to see what her next play might be.

Her gaze is still trained on mine as she slips her hands beneath the waistband of her maternity pants. My cock strains against my own pants as I watch her drag them down her thighs, pulling her panties with them. She bends over, her stomach causing some restriction as she stops with them by her ankles.

"Let me," I tell her, dropping down to my knees as I

reach for her pants. Sliding my fingers through the material, I hold them open as she places her hands on my shoulders and removes her feet from them. I lift my eyes, my gaze traveling along her thighs, her pussy, over her stomach and tits, until I meet her heated stare. "Goddamn, look at you."

Her lips part, a choppy breath escaping her.

"I'm on my knees for you, baby." My voice is hoarse as I drag my fingertips along the insides of her thighs. "Let me worship you."

She lets out a soft moan, her eyelids fluttering shut as my fingers drift over her cunt. "I don't know. Do you think you've been good enough?"

"Fuck, I hope so," I groan, a rush of warmth going directly to my dick. "I'm always a good boy for you. I'll do whatever you want me to do if it means I can taste you."

"Whatever I want?" she questions me, raising an eyebrow as she runs her hands through my hair. "I like you like this, on your knees." She pulls her bottom lip between her teeth. "What if I told you I wanted to hear you beg?"

Sliding my hands along the backs of her thighs, I push her legs backward with my chest, her knees bending as she drops down onto the bed. "Then I'll fucking beg," I growl as I lean forward, gently laying her back on the mattress. "Although, I'd much rather use my mouth to make you come."

"Then do it," she murmurs, parting her thighs as she

looks at me over her swollen stomach. "Stop talking and make me come."

Goddamn, I love her like this, demanding what she wants from me.

Her green eyes are filled with need and anticipation as she rakes her teeth across her bottom lip. I wait for her next command, but she doesn't say anything as she runs her fingers through my hair, guiding me down until I'm burying my face between her legs. Her grip tightens on my hair as my tongue slips out and I lick her, flattening my tongue as I reach her clit.

Her hips buck, instantly lifting from the bed as I suck her clit between my lips. A moan escapes her, my name falling from her lips as I pin her down against the bed, working my mouth against her. My tongue circles around her lips, sucking on the tender part of her body before I release it. I fuck her with my mouth, licking her cunt, tasting her on my tongue before teasing her clit again.

My forearms press against the inside of her thighs, holding her in place as my fingertips dig into her flesh. I feast upon her, tasting, teasing, licking, and fucking. Releasing her leg with one arm, I move my hand along her flesh until my fingers are pressing against her.

I slowly push a finger inside of her, feeling how tight she is around me. "I can't wait to see how my wife looks taking my cock instead of my finger."

Riley moans again, her breathing ragged and

shallow and her pussy clenching around my finger instantly.

"Mmm," I murmur against her clit, feeling my cock twitch from the sound of her. "You like that, don't you?"

"Yes," she admits breathlessly.

I can feel her growing tense beneath my hands and my mouth. My tongue swirls around her clit, over and over, applying more pressure as my finger fucks her tight hole. My balls constrict, drawing closer to my body as I feel her pussy tightening around me.

Jesus Christ, I need my cock inside her before I come in my pants.

Riley moans louder, her fingers tangled in my hair as she lifts her hips to meet me before I withdraw my finger. I lick her again, my tongue landing on her clit once more. Moving the other hand along her thigh, I slip it between her legs, pushing my finger into her. I pump it a few times before adding another, stroking the insides of her cunt as I lap at her clit.

"Oh god, oh god," she moans, the sound transforming as she cries out. She tightens around me, her body jerking as her orgasm hits her with full force. "Nash, Nash, Nash," she half breathes, half moans my name like she's whispering a prayer.

I'll answer every fucking prayer she has.

I don't stop fucking her with my mouth until she's done riding out the waves of ecstasy. Only then do I pull my mouth away, still tasting her on my tongue as I wipe the dampness from my lips. Riley lifts her head to look at me as I rise to my feet. Her eyes are glazed over and she's fully satiated from her orgasm.

"I could spend the rest of my life buried between your legs."

A lazy grin pulls on her lips. "Well, we would get nothing done if you spent the rest of your life there."

"True," I say, a smirk pulling on my lips as I reach for her, my fingers trailing over her skin. "If I kept my face there, I'd never get to bury my cock inside of you."

"Why are you still dressed?" she questions me, her voice thick with need. "Are you going to fuck me or not?"

A chuckle escapes me and I can't get undressed quick enough. "I thought you'd never ask," I retort as I toss my shirt on the floor and drop my hands to my pants. I slide them down my thighs, along with my boxer briefs, my cock hard as a fucking rock as I kick off my pants and stand completely naked in front of her.

Her eyes widen and she slowly moves into a sitting position as she reaches for me. "When did you get these?" she asks, her voice curious and filled with lust as she wraps her hand around my length, stroking the barbells on the underside.

I lift an eyebrow at her, watching her as she looks at my Jacob's ladder. "You say it like you've seen me without them."

Riley's eyes flash to mine, a pink tint creeping across her cheeks. My mouth twitches as I watch the embarrassment dance across her face, never mind the fact that we're both completely naked and I just fucked her with my mouth.

"What aren't you telling me?"

"You don't remember, do you?" Her tongue darts out to wet her lips. "I saw you naked during my senior year. You were home for the summer and you left the bathroom door ajar."

"Were you watching me?"

The thought alone has me ready to come.

Riley shakes her head at me, her tits moving with the movement. "No. I peeked in through the crack and as soon as I saw your dick, I looked away."

"Oh, wait, I do remember. I didn't know you saw me, though." I pause for a moment, my hand wrapping around hers as I start to move her along the length of my cock. "You should have come in. We wouldn't have had to wait this long." Her fingers move along the barbells, the friction a delicious pleasure. "Do you want to feel these inside of you?"

"God, yes," she breathes, her gaze going from my cock to my eyes. "I want to feel every inch of you inside of me."

"Tell me how we're doing this, love," I half groan, my voice hoarse and my cock throbbing for her. "I don't want to hurt you."

"Well, I've never done this before." She lets go of me, rising to her feet as she starts to turn around, showing me her perfect ass. "I read somewhere that doggy style can be the best when your stomach is this big."

"Climb onto the bed," I tell her, running my hand along her spine as I urge her forward. "Show me your pretty pussy so I can fuck my wife from behind."

Riley inhales sharply as she obeys and crawls onto the bed on her hands and knees until her ass is in the air for me. I walk up to her, my fingers trailing over her flesh as I position my cock against her cunt. Riley pushes back against me, slowly impaling herself on my length. I thrust my hips forward, pressing into her until my dick is fully inside her.

"Fuck, you feel amazing," I moan, my hands roaming over her lower back, down to her ass as I start to piston my hips, easing in and out of her. "One day I'm going to fuck this ass too," I tell her, my fingers coasting across her cheeks. "I'm going to fuck every single one of your holes over and over."

"Nash," she breathes, my name sounding like a whimper falling from her lips as she presses her ass back against me.

"You feel your cunt stretching around me?" I murmur, my hand traveling up her spine until I'm wrapping her hair around it. I pull her head back slightly, pushing into her again. "You feel my piercings rubbing your insides?"

"Don't stop," she moans, her eyelids fluttering shut. "Fuck me harder."

I pause momentarily, my heart thumping in my chest. "It won't hurt the baby, will it?"

She looks at me over her shoulder. "No."

"Okay, good." I let out a sigh of relief, one hand grabbing her hip while the other holds on to her hair as I start to fuck her again. I move my hips, pumping my cock in and out of her. My thrusts grow faster and more urgent, harder and demanding. "Goddamn, you take my cock like you were made for it."

Riley takes every single thrust, meeting me as she presses her ass against me. Her chest falls forward, her face pressed against the mattress as I pound into her. "Nash, I'm so close already. Please don't stop. Oh my god, don't stop."

"That's it, baby," I groan, a warmth building in the pit of my stomach. My balls constrict, drawing closer to my body. "Come all over my cock."

"Come with me," she pleads, her head lifting as her eyes meet mine. Her pussy clenches around me, her walls quaking around my cock as her orgasm erupts. "Please."

That's all it takes to send me over the edge. I pump my hips, pounding into her over and over as I spill my cum deep inside her. I fuck her until we're both completely spent with nothing left to give.

I slowly pull out of her, watching her as she rolls onto her side, completely breathless and in a daze. I leave her for a moment and head to the bathroom to get something to clean her up with. Riley looks at me as I walk back in and climb onto the bed with her. Her gaze is soft, watching me as I take care of her.

I toss the washcloth onto the floor with our clothes, my hand trailing over her stomach as I look back at her. Fuck, I love seeing her like this. It's intoxicating and addicting.

Riley moves over, pulling the blanket out from under her body, but she can't cover herself completely because I'm still on it. She gives me a look. "Can I get covered or would you prefer I freeze?"

A smirk lifts my lips. "I can keep you warm, wife."

"Yeah, you can… if you get off the damn blanket," she retorts, jerking on the blanket again.

Laughter escapes me as I roll off the bed and pull the covers away from her in an effort to try and cover her completely, but instead, I leave her bare to the cold air.

Riley gasps, her eyes wide before she glares at me. "Nash Simmons."

"I didn't mean to do that!" I laugh again, quickly climbing onto the bed behind her as I pull the blankets back over us. "Is that better?"

She presses her back against me, her head nestling against the pillow as I wrap my arm around her, holding her to the front of my body. "Much."

"I'll keep you warm all through the night."

"Good boy," she yawns, her hand finding mine as she threads our fingers together. "You know good boys get rewarded."

Goddamn, I'm obsessed with her.

"I can't wait to find out what it is."

Riley laughs quietly but she doesn't respond as she begins to drift off to sleep. I hold her close to me, feeling her heart beating in her chest, listening to the sound of her breathing.

She is the only reward I want.

CHAPTER TWENTY-THREE
RILEY

My arms stretch upward, my spine lengthening as I slowly peel my eyes open, squinting against the harsh light shining through the window. As I move, I feel a warm solid body behind me, momentarily catching me by surprise until my mind registers that it's him.

Almost every night the past month, I've intentionally fallen asleep on the couch with Nash, mainly because I didn't want to go to bed without him, but I also didn't want to cross that line and ask him to sleep with me.

I didn't have to ask last night.

He stayed all night long.

His tattooed arm snakes over my torso, his fingers dancing across my naked, swollen stomach. "Mm," he murmurs, his face nuzzling against my hair. "I could get used to this."

"Used to what?" I ask him, my voice quiet as I nestle my head in the pillow. My breath hitches, catching in my throat as anticipation swirls in my stomach.

"Waking up with you next to me."

My heart stumbles over itself in my chest as the sound of his voice vibrates against my eardrums. His warmth encapsulates me, soothing my soul as I turn in his arms to face him. Nash looks at me—really looks at me—before pulling my face to his chest. I breathe in the scent of him, reveling in the way he feels and the way he makes me feel.

From the nightstand behind Nash comes the annoying sound of his alarm. He groans, removing one arm from me as he reaches behind himself to turn it off. "I don't want to leave again. I feel like I just got back."

"I know, but you have to," I tell him, refusing to be the reason why he doesn't do the things he's supposed to do. "I'll be here when you get back home."

"You make it so hard to leave," he murmurs as he buries his face against my neck. "I just want to spend the rest of eternity right here with you."

"Well, we can't do that," I tell him, laughing as I wrap my arms around him. "When the baby comes, we're going to have to answer to him." My heart stops in my chest as Nash pulls back to look me in the eye. "I don't know why I said that. I meant me. I'm going to have to answer to him."

His throat bobs, his eyes burning through mine as he shakes his head at me. "Not just you, love," he says quietly as he moves closer, pressing his lips to my forehead. "We both will."

"Nash," I whisper his name, emotion building in my throat as he moves in the bed, his eyes meeting mine once more. "He's not your responsibility."

"What if I told you I want him to be?" He pauses as he slowly sits up in bed. "Every child should have a father figure in their life. He doesn't have to biologically be my child for me to fill that role."

My eyes widen in shock, desperately searching his. "Please, don't, Nash."

"Don't what?" he asks as he rises to his feet, collecting his dirty clothes from the floor.

"Don't say things like that," I tell him as I start to move to sit up when a sudden, sharp pain radiates from my temple. My face screws up, my eyes closing as I wince.

He stops, his clothes in his hands as concern moves across his expression. "Are you okay?"

I nod, squinting my eyes as the pain subsides and becomes more of an ache. "Yeah. Changing positions just made my head hurt a little."

"Are you sure you're okay?" His voice is hoarse with panic laced within his words. "Do you want me to call the doctor?"

"Nash, I'm fine," I tell him, ignoring the dull ache settling behind my eyes. "Can I ask you to do something for me?"

"Anything," he says in a rush, worry still lingering in his tone.

"Don't tell me things to make me feel good when you don't know what your future holds."

The muscle in his jaw tightens, his eyes staring directly into my soul. "Do you want to know what I see when I think about my future?"

"Yes."

I don't hesitate to answer even though it scares the shit out of me. I can't live my life in fear of getting hurt anymore. I want to know. *I need to know.*

"You." He says the word with declaration, like it's the written law. "You are all I see, Riley. You're all I've ever seen." He moves back to me, kissing my forehead once more. "I'll see you when I get home."

Home.

It sounds so natural falling from his lips, like this is where he's always belonged. Right here, with me. Three words linger on the tip of my tongue, but I swallow them back before they escape me. I watch Nash as he leaves my bedroom, stopping by the bathroom and the guest room before he makes his way downstairs.

He's barely gone two minutes when my phone dings from my nightstand. Leaning forward, I reach for it, seeing his name on the screen.

> NASH
>
> I ordered you breakfast and it should be there in twenty minutes.

> **RILEY**
>
> You didn't have to do that.

> **NASH**
>
> I didn't have time to make you food and I need to make sure my girl eats.
>
> You're growing a whole-ass human in your stomach right now, so nutrition is important.

My eyes won't stop drifting back to those two little words. *My girl.* After the conversation we had before he left and the things he admitted, it's hard not to read into it. He could mean so much by it, but in my heart and soul, I know exactly what he means.

I've always been his, even if we were too stubborn and blind to see it until now.

Nash Simmons was always the one person I wanted, but when we were younger, it would have never worked out. He went through the typical phase of sleeping around and I ended up dating a guy for the last two years of high school. Nash was traveling for hockey, chasing his dreams while trying to get into a professional league.

I knew I needed to let the thought of him go, even if I hated to do it. I couldn't hold on to a crush that I didn't realize was actually reciprocated.

I didn't want to upset my best friend by having a thing for her brother, so I hid my feelings and locked them away inside, swearing I would never revisit them again. When he started playing professionally, it made things a little easier. At first, I didn't see him as much and I convinced myself there would never be anything.

Nash had to be seeing other women, so I started to do the same, although none of them ever stuck. None of them ever lasted because they were never him. I decided to spend time alone and spent two years single before I met Chad. That was short-lived and we've seen where that situation got me.

If I'm being honest, as much as I feel like we wasted so much time getting to this point, I wouldn't redo it. If I never met Chad, I wouldn't be blessed with this little boy who's going to make me a mom. He's the biggest blessing life has brought me.

I don't know the extent of Nash's dating history and I don't even care at this point. All that matters is now and the moments we have together. He may not want me tomorrow or next week or next year even, but he wants me now and that's enough for me.

He's enough for me.

CHAPTER TWENTY-FOUR

NASH

"Fuck, I missed you."

Riley smiles at me, setting her book down as I stand in the doorway staring at her for a moment. Even though I was only gone for two days, I swear it felt like a fucking lifetime. We got back a lot later than anticipated and Riley texted me earlier to tell me she would be in bed reading.

"Come here," she says, motioning for me to join her on the bed. My feet instantly move without any instruction and I climb onto the mattress, not getting under the covers in my street clothes. "I'm glad you're home."

"So am I," I admit, pulling her into my arms as I bury my face in her neck, breathing in her scent. Riley Harris consumes every single one of my thoughts. When I'm not with her, that's exactly where I want to be.

She's my drug of choice and I'm hopelessly addicted.

"I watched your game," she says softly, her cheek moving against my chest. "It seems like you behaved out there."

A chuckle escapes me. "Well, if I remember correctly, a certain someone told me that I get rewarded if I behave." A smirk pulls on my lips and I lift my face to look at hers. "Then again, I was promised punishment too, so maybe I should have been a bad boy."

"Which would you prefer?" she asks, her voice soft as she trails her fingertips along the sides of my biceps and up over my shoulders. "A reward or a punishment?"

"Well, this is a little unexpected," I tell her, my voice thick with need as my cock instantly starts to grow. My eyes slowly search hers. "You must have really missed me, huh? Or perhaps what you really missed was my cock."

"You wish." A ghost of a smile dances across her lips as she sits up. "I have toys to take care of my needs."

As soon as she says the words, I expect there to be a pink tint dancing across her cheeks, but there is none. There's not a single look of shyness in her expression. She stands by exactly what she says without any embarrassment.

Not only am I curious as hell, but I'm turned on more than ever with the confidence radiating from her.

"Where are they?" I question her, sitting up with her.

She raises an eyebrow. "Why? Do you want to borrow them?"

She's so fucking feisty sometimes, I love it.

A chuckle vibrates in my chest as I reach for her, pulling her close as I begin to push the hem of her shirt up over her swollen stomach. "I do want to borrow them," I tell her as she lets me lift her shirt away from her body. I toss it onto the floor, my fingers trailing over her full breasts. "I don't want to use them on myself, though."

"Oh yeah?" she says, mimicking my movements as she strips my shirt away from me. Her fingers slip beneath the waistband of my pants, her hand not stopping until her fingertips dance over the shaft of my cock. "Who are you going to use them on?"

"You," I tell her, gently pushing her back onto the bed. My hands find her shorts, pulling them and her panties down her thighs, her calves, and past her feet before I toss them onto the floor. I remove my own pants and underwear, kicking them to the side as I walk along the side of her bed, my hands roaming over her warm skin.

"They're in the bottom drawer of my nightstand."

A smirk lifts my lips and I bend down, pulling open the drawer as I find a healthy assortment of toys. "Which one is your favorite?"

"The dark pink one."

"Mm," I groan as I take out the small case and flip it open, pulling out the vibrator. Turning back to Riley, I climb onto the bed with her as I hand it to her. "Show me what you like, love."

Her eyes meet mine in a flash, her gaze leveling on my own. Her lips part, almost as if she's going to argue, but instead she presses a button, turning it on as she selects the vibration setting she wants. She rolls onto her side, slowly parting her legs as she takes the vibrator and begins to trail it over her body.

My eyes follow along with the device, watching her nipples instantly harden from it. My cock throbs, wetness growing on the tip as I watch her slowly bringing it farther down her body. She pauses as she reaches between her legs, her gaze glued on mine the entire time.

"I need the lube."

My breath catches in my throat and I shake my head at her, lowering myself on the bed. "I'll get you wet." Spreading her legs further apart, I bury my face between her thighs, drawing saliva onto my tongue before spitting on her. She lets out a low moan as soon as it hits her.

I pull my head back the slightest, my eyes meeting hers once more. "Now show me how you fuck yourself when I'm not around to do it for you."

She inhales sharply, moving the vibrator along her pussy, sliding one side of it in. I watch her move with rapt attention, her wrists moving back and forth as she pumps the silicone in and out of her tight cunt. Her lips part, ragged breaths escaping her as she continues to move it. On the other end of it, there's a small suction spot, but she doesn't position it over her clit.

She looks fucking sexy as hell, laying like this on the bed, fucking herself while I watch her. Pre-cum drips from my cock and I lean forward, moving closer to her. My tongue finds her clit and I begin to move it around the sensitive area, tasting and teasing her while she continues to pump the vibrator in and out.

Riley moves against my face, her hands finding my hair as she pulls me away from her pussy. Her eyes meet mine and the intensity in them sends a shock of electricity directly to my dick. "Fuck me, Nash." She removes the vibrator, flipping it around so the suction is near her pussy. "I want you to fuck me and use this at the same time."

She doesn't have to say another fucking word.

Moving behind her, I lie down on the bed so I'm spooning her, positioning the head of my cock against her. Riley pushes back, my dick sinking deep inside of her as I thrust into her with my hips. A groan escapes me at the same time she moans.

Riley moves the toy into my hand, guiding me toward her clit with the suction part. "Here," she says quietly as I slowly start to move my hips. She lifts her top leg a little higher. "I like it right here," she murmurs, positioning it in the perfect spot. The device suctions around her clit, simulating lips and a tongue playing with her. "Mmm," she moans, her head falling back onto the bed. "Yes, just like that, Nash."

I fall into a rhythm, holding on to her as I hold the toy against her clit, instantly feeling her clenching around my cock. "Not so fast, love," I murmur, pulling the vibrator away from her. Riley groans in protest. "I didn't tell you that you could come yet."

"I want to come," she says, half pleading as I continue to fuck her. "It feels so good with you inside me at the same time."

"You'll come when I tell you that you can."

My fingertips dig into her flesh as I begin to piston my hips, fucking her harder. I watch her tits as they begin to jiggle from the movement. Riley's hand reaches back, grabbing my thigh as I start to move faster, working my cock inside of her. The walls of her cunt grip the barbells on the underside of my dick, creating the most delicious friction.

"Goddamn, you're fucking sexy," I murmur, my eyes and fingers trailing over her skin as I continue to move inside of her. "You take my cock so well, don't you, wife?"

"Yes," she moans, her pussy clenching around my length. I smile at her reactions to me calling her that again. "Please let me come, Nash."

"Is that what you want, baby?"

"Yes," she begs as she presses herself back against me with more force, meeting each and every one of my thrusts. "Please."

"Fuck, you're perfect. I love the way you beg while you're taking every inch of me." Grabbing the toy, I slide it into Riley's hand, pushing it between her legs. "I want you to make yourself come all over my cock."

Riley moves it back over her clit, the sucking motion instantly making her clench around me. "Oh god, Nash."

"That's it, mama." I shift my hips, slamming into her as a string of moans and ragged breaths fall from her lips. Her face screws up, her lips parting as she's hanging on the edge of pleasure, and her eyes flash to mine, needing that last command. My balls constrict instantly.

"Come."

She cries out as she shatters around me, completely losing herself as her orgasm hits her with full force. All it takes is to feel her clenching around me, moaning my name, to send me over the edge with her. I spill myself into her, slowly fucking her until we're fully satiated and she's filled with my cum.

I slowly ease out of her, lying behind her for a moment as we catch our breaths. The vibrator lies on the bed beside her, buzzing around on the mattress as she struggles to regulate her breathing. Leaning over her, I grab it and turn it off, but Riley takes it from me before she heads into the bathroom.

She comes back into the room and I'm transfixed by the way she looks right now. She's completely naked, her hand instinctively drifting across her stomach. Her gaze meets mine and she walks toward me, climbing in front of me on the bed.

I wrap my arm around her and we lie in a comfortable silence as I bury my face against her neck. My hand trails over her stomach, my fingers stroking her skin.

"How soon after you have him do you think you'll be ready for another baby?"

She's quiet for a second and I wonder if she fell asleep.

"What?"

A smirk pulls on my lips. "I've always imagined fucking you, but doing it while you're pregnant is a whole different fantasy I never knew I had." I press my lips against the nape of her neck. "After you have him, I want to put a baby in your belly."

"You're insane," she says after a moment, a soft laugh escaping her. Sleep hangs heavily in her voice and she lets out a yawn. "You know that, right?"

"One day, Riley," I promise, murmuring the words against her skin.

"You're crazy," she says, her voice barely audible as her breathing grows even and she starts to drift off.

"Crazy for you," I tell her, but I'm not sure if she hears me. I relish the way she feels, naked and pressed against me. She just fits and I know this is all I want.

This is all I'll *ever* want.

CHAPTER TWENTY-FIVE
RILEY

Squinting my eyes, I attempt to find some kind of relief from the nagging pain in my head. It's been lingering for a few days now and no matter what I take for it, it just doesn't seem to help. It may dull the ache a bit, but it still lingers. My body feels exhausted from fighting against it, and I resist the urge to just curl up on the couch with a pillow and blanket.

As I head into the kitchen, a smile lifts my lips when I see a bouquet of flowers sitting on the table. I don't know when Nash put them there with how busy his day was with their morning skate and game-day routine. He left about a few hours ago when I was lying down to take a nap. The guys rotate whose house they're having their pre-game meal at and today it is at Rowan's house.

I haven't been feeling well since I woke up this morning and spent most of the day in bed. Nash was concerned when he left, but I assured him I was fine. He insisted I stay home during tonight's game so I can rest and I didn't object to the idea.

As I go to move toward where the flowers are, the strangest thing happens as I turn my head. The light shining above in the kitchen leaves a long trail, moving with my line of sight.

I blink three times, my vision returning to normal as I walk over to the table to smell the flowers. It's the prettiest arrangement and I find a small card tucked inside.

> *If I remember correctly, when you first opened your flower shop, you told me that carnations are your favorite.*
> *I hope they still are.*
> *See you tonight.*
> *Love, Nash*

I read over his words two more times before tucking the small card back into the flowers. As I stare at them for a moment, I run my hand over my stomach, an unusual feeling engulfing me as I realize I haven't felt the baby move at all today. I push my palm firmly against my belly where I know part of his body is. He doesn't react at first, but I'm relieved when I feel him pushing back.

Moving slowly, I turn back around to the counter,

my eyes doing the same thing with the trails of light. A sigh escapes me, worry rolling in the pit of my stomach as I let my eyelids fall shut once more, attempting to get my vision to cooperate.

I don't know what the hell is going on, but all of this is extremely unusual for me. None of the symptoms of PoTS have ever been like this. Abandoning the idea of eating any food, I move over to the other side of the counter where the small blood pressure cuff is and I slide it over my wrist as I find the paperwork the doctor gave me with different symptoms to keep an eye out for.

My eyes scan the paper as I feel the cuff squeezing my arm. Every single symptom I've been experiencing is written as clear as day on this paper.

Fuck. This isn't good at all.

The blood pressure cuff deflates and beeps at me. I glance at it, expecting to see a number on it, but instead there's an error message. My eyebrows scrunch as I press the button and try again, waiting for it to work this time, but it does the same exact thing.

I glance at the time on the stove. It's already six o'clock in the evening. I don't know how the hell I lost so much time today. My body feels bogged down, almost like I'm coming down with the flu. That has to be it, but out of caution, I decide to dial the on-call number for the ob-gyn office.

A woman answers, taking my information before telling me that she'll pass my details on to the doctor who is on call and they will give me a call back within the next twenty minutes. Anxiety builds in the pit of my stomach as I halt, standing in shock in my kitchen for a moment.

I'm only thirty-seven weeks. According to the doctors and the baby books, a baby could come at this point and be fine, but the longer they are in there, the better. I run my hand over my stomach again. He's not ready to come out yet. Hell, I'm not sure I'm ready for him to come yet either.

My movements are slow, my head still aching, as I climb the stairs up to the nursery. It feels like I'm climbing a damn mountain with the way my legs feel like they're weighing me down. I'm a bit panicked and not feeling well at all as I find the packed hospital bag sitting on the dresser. I open it up, looking through everything once again.

Everything is in there and ready to go. I run my hands over the newborn-sized outfit, my eyes landing on the small jersey from Nash sitting next to it. I lift it up, flipping it over, as I see BABY with Nash's number on it.

Tears spring to my eyes, but I quickly swallow back my emotion as my phone starts to vibrate in the pocket of my sweatpants. I pull it out, my heart pounding in my chest as I see it's the on-call number. I answer it in a rush, quickly slipping into a conversation with the doctor that does not go where I wanted it to.

She wants me to come into the hospital, even if it's

just for them to check me out and send me home… but she also tells me to bring my hospital bag just in case.

Fear envelops me and I'm momentarily frozen as my heart kicks into overdrive. Dread rolls in the pit of my stomach and I shove the jersey into my bag before zipping it up and heading into my bedroom. I'm moving on autopilot, fueled by the adrenaline coursing through my body. I didn't have a bag packed for myself, so I quickly grab a few things and toiletries and shove them into a duffle bag before heading down to the foyer.

The fucking car seat isn't even in my car yet.

I'm not ready for this. I'm not prepared at all.

Closing my eyes, I take a deep breath, controlling myself as I focus on my breathing, counting the inhales and exhales. I need to get it together here. Everything is going to be fine. I don't need to call Nash and worry him or anyone else. I just need to get myself to the hospital, so they can check me out and send me home.

If only it were that simple…

***

"Did anyone come here with you?" The nurse, Hadley, questions me as she secures an admission band around my wrist. "I can go out and get someone to take them to your room."

I shake my head, my mind paralyzed in fear and shock. "I came by myself."

Her eyes widen. "You drove yourself here?"

Pulling the inside of my cheek between my teeth, I nod. "I thought I would be in and out of here."

"I'm sorry," she says softly, her hand reaching for mine as she gives me a gentle, reassuring squeeze. "I wish we were able to, but I'm afraid we can't, given the circumstances."

When I arrived, my blood pressure was alarmingly high. So high the nurse immediately went in search of a doctor and they made the decision to admit me. It's exactly what we were all hoping wouldn't happen—severe preeclampsia. The headaches and distortion to my vision is caused by the swelling in my brain. It's too risky and unsafe for them to send me home, especially with the reduced activity of the baby.

He's being affected by this now too.

I will do whatever I have to, to keep him safe.

The doctor comes back into the room, her face grim as she walks over to the computer and pulls up my lab results. "The protein in your urine is alarmingly high." She glances at me, realizing I'm not understanding. "It's caused by the high blood pressure, and that combined with the results from your blood work, your kidneys are now being affected."

The dread in the pit of my stomach feels like a bag of concrete.

"Given your neurological symptoms, we want to make sure you don't end up having a seizure or a stroke. As soon as we get you into your room, we will start a few different medications. One will be to induce labor and another will be to prevent any seizures."

My eyes widen and my voice cracks. "Induce labor?"

"Unfortunately, your condition is not good and delivery is the only treatment for preeclampsia. If we can keep you stabilized and the baby doesn't go into distress, we are planning for a natural delivery. If any additional issues arise that threaten you and the baby's safety, we will have to take you in for an emergency C-section."

All of this is extremely jarring, leaving nothing but fear inside of me. I know she's only telling me so I'm well-informed, but Jesus Christ. When I first started having a headache the other day, I didn't realize this is what it would lead to. I had no idea I would be sitting in the hospital with my life potentially on the line.

I would rather know all of this than be blindsided by it.

"Okay," I tell her, putting on my brave face as I nod. "Whatever has to happen to keep him safe."

In the back of my mind, I know they prioritize the health of the mother, but I can't focus on that. I would rather have him alive and me not here than to have to live in this world without the precocious little life I grew inside my abdomen.

The doctor tells me she'll be by to check on me after they get me settled and the medications started. Hadley turns back to me, an apologetic, yet comforting smile on her face.

"Let's get you transferred to your room." She starts to move about the room, unhooking things from the wall to get me moved. "If you want to call someone to come be with you, we can get them to your room too." She gives me a knowing look. "We're going to just pretend you didn't drive yourself here in the condition you're in."

I wince, giving her a silent apology. "In my defense, I didn't want to worry anyone else. I didn't think it was this serious."

"Well, it's just a good thing you came in when you did," she tells me, her voice soft, and I don't miss the hint of worry lingering. Hadley leaves the room for a moment and I quickly pull out my phone, tapping on my messages as I find the thread with Nova.

Riley: I don't want you to worry, but I started to feel pretty shitty this afternoon, so I called the doctors and they asked me to come to the hospital. They just admitted me, but I am okay and the baby is okay.

Nova doesn't text me back, instead she calls me immediately.

"What's going on?" she questions me as soon as I answer her call.

I give her a quick rundown from the doctor, leaving out the super-scary parts like about having a seizure or a stroke. The last thing I want to do is send her into a panic. I'll explain how serious it is when she gets here.

"I just texted Nonna and she's coming here now to stay with Poe. I'll be there in, like, thirty minutes, okay?"

"Okay," I tell her, emotion encapsulating me as I rub my hand over my stomach, wishing he would just move. "I didn't say anything to Nash."

"Don't," she says, her voice serious, and I know why. The last thing he needs is any type of distraction. "I will tell him after the game."

"Okay," I repeat, nodding my head and forcing a smile as the nurse comes back into the room. "They're getting ready to transfer me now, so I will text you the room number when I'm there."

"I love you, Ry. Everything will be okay, I promise."

"I love you too," I tell her, ending the call as I look back at the nurse with tears in my eyes. I know Nova will be here soon enough, but it is terrifying being here alone.

"Are you ready?"

I nod at her, not feeling ready at all, but knowing I have no choice. I'm a mess of emotions, filled with fear and worry, but there's nothing I can do about any of it. I want Nash here, but that's another thing that's beyond my control.

All I can do now is be brave and hope that the doctors can keep both the baby and me safe.

Both of our lives depend on it.

CHAPTER TWENTY-SIX

NASH

The energy in the air is palpable as we come off the ice and head back into the locker room. We just won 5–0 and the entire game was intense. We scored two goals in the first period and after we came back for the second, things started to get pretty physical and chippy. Much to my dismay, I managed to get through the game without getting into any fights, although I did end up shoving one of the defensemen on the other team.

"Good game tonight, boys," Caleb tells all of us as everyone finds their spots and starts to get undressed. Caleb pulls off his jersey, tossing it onto the bench as he looks around the room at all of us. He goes into his speech, giving a recap and a rundown of the good points. It's something we do after every game and tonight, he hands the team belt—much like a wrestling belt—to the player of the game, Rowan.

"You played your fucking ass off tonight, Taylor," Caleb says, clapping his shoulder as he hands him the belt. "I don't know how you made some of the saves you did, but you were like a goddamn ninja out there."

Rowan laughs loudly, holding the belt up as he looks around the room at all of us. "Okay, I did play my ass off, but so did the rest of you. I didn't make any goals tonight and we wouldn't have won without that too." He smiles, showing his bright white teeth, his blue eyes filled with happiness. "Great fucking game, boys."

Everyone starts clapping, some of the guys hooting and hollering as we all cheer him on. Carson jumps up and down, his excitement like that of a little kid. You would think we just won the Cup or something, but no —it was just a regular season game.

Every win, every point helps us keep the number one seed in our division. We're heading into playoff territory soon enough, so it's vital that we keep this energy going and keep moving forward like this.

After removing my gear, I grab my phone from my locker, turning it on to check it before heading into the shower. As the screen turns on, I see there are multiple messages from Nova, along with a few voicemails. Panic immediately floods me and my heart stops immediately in my chest as my phone gives me a preview of her messages.

> NOVA
> Nash, I need you to call me as soon as you see this.

NOVA

It's Riley.

NOVA

I'm here at the hospital with her. She's okay right now, but things aren't good.

NOVA

The baby's in distress and Riley is getting worse.

NOVA

FUCKING CALL ME.

I don't hesitate, tapping on her name immediately. My breath is lodged in my throat and my heart refuses to beat. Time is suspended and it feels like a fucking lifetime when she finally answers on the last ring.

"Nash, you need to get here as soon as you can."

"What the fuck is going on?" I question her, my voice tense, yet filled with worry. I practically yell the words, my heart immediately kicking into overdrive as it pounds erratically against my rib cage. "Is Riley okay? Is the baby okay?"

Nova is silent for a moment. Caleb appears beside me, Lincoln right behind him. I look at the two of them, seeing Rowan and Carson as they move closer, but I don't truly see them—not right now. "I don't know, Nash. Things just started to go downhill so fast." I can hear the panic in her voice, the emotion consuming her. "They said they needed to get her into surgery immediately and just took her back." She chokes on a sob. "Please just get here."

"I'm on my way."

I end the call, shoving the phone in my pocket as I start to rifle through my locker, looking for my keys. I'm moving in a rush, panic fueling my body as my heart can't control itself. My breathing is ragged and erratic.

"What's going on, Nash?"

"They just took Riley back for an emergency C-section," I bark at whomever spoke. I don't bother looking at either of them as my fingers finally feel the key fob for my car and my wallet. "I have to go."

"I'll drive you," Caleb interjects, his hand landing on my shoulder. "You're in no condition to drive right now."

"I'm fine," I tell him, turning around to face him. My hands are shaking, my entire body feeling like I'm going to crawl out of my skin from feeling so fucking helpless. "I need to get there now."

"This isn't up for debate," Caleb says, his voice stern as he spins me around, pushing me toward the door.

"I'm coming with you," Lincoln says without hesitation, his footsteps rushing as he leaves the room with us.

"So are we," Caleb and Rowan both say at the same time, following after us.

It's a fucking whirlwind, and I'm lost in my head and feelings as we all pile into Caleb's car. He drives like he races cars for a living, and I'm not even sure how we get there in one piece. I can't focus on any of it and the entire ride is a blur before he's pulling the car to an abrupt halt in front of the hospital.

We're not even at a full stop as I'm shoving open my door, my feet hitting the ground running. I rush through the automatic sliding glass doors as they part, not stopping until I reach the front desk. "Where is she?" I knock my fist on the counter like a fucking psycho. "Where is Riley?"

The woman at the desk lifts her gaze to mine, her forehead creasing. "I'm sorry—"

"WHERE IS MY FUCKING WIFE?!"

I hear Rowan's voice behind me. "His wife?" he half whispers to one of the guys.

"I don't know," I hear another voice, but I don't pay attention to who it is.

"May I have her name, please?"

My lips part as I go to tell her, when I see a flurry of wild blonde curly hair to my right.

"Oh my god, Nash." Nova breathes a sigh of relief as she reaches for my arm. I turn to look at her, watching her face crumble as soon as she sees me. "Thank God you're here."

I pull my sister into my arms, holding her as sobs rack her body. I swallow back my own emotions, knowing I can't break right now too. "What's going on? Where is she?"

"She's in surgery right now. I've been waiting for someone to come back and give me an update."

My eyes are wild as I spin back to the woman at the front desk. "Why hasn't the doctor come out? I need to speak to whomever is in charge of her care."

Her eyes widen, filling with concern as she glances at her two colleagues who are now standing behind her, most likely because of the chaos I'm causing out here.

"Sir, we're going to have to ask you to calm down or we will have to have you escorted out of here."

"I'll calm down when someone tells me where the hell my wife is and what's going on with her and the baby."

The double doors behind Nova are pushed open and a man walks out dressed in surgical scrubs and gown. The top of his head is covered using a cap and a mask is pulled down beneath his chin. "Are you Riley Harris's husband?"

"Yes."

Nova gasps and murmurs erupt from the guys behind me. "What?"

I glance at my sister. "I will explain later."

"Are all of you family too?" he asks my sister and the guys.

"Yes," they all say in unison without a second thought.

"Very well," he says, nodding as he motions for us to follow him. "We have a private family waiting room you can all come to." He looks at me as we reach the door. I go to step inside, but his hand darts out to stop me. "Not you. You can come with me."

Dread rolls in the pit of my stomach and I fold my lips between my teeth, nodding at him before looking at my sister. Her teary eyes are filled with fear. I pull her in for a quick hug, releasing her as Lincoln steps up behind her. "I'll update you as soon as I know what's going on."

Nova gives me a quick nod, and I leave them all behind as I follow the doctor through the double doors. We walk through the hallway, and he leads me into a separate waiting room outside of the surgical unit.

He motions for me to take a seat, but I shake my head, insisting on standing. He gives me a knowing look. "You can sit down. They're both okay."

Relief floods me and I instantly feel like I can breathe. I'm reluctant to sit but I do.

He takes a seat across from me. "Surgery went well. We were able to deliver the baby without any issues. He was a little sluggish initially at birth due to the medications Riley received, but with a little support with his breathing, he quickly rebounded, and is happy and healthy."

"Thank God," I breathe the words, my throat constricting as my eyes begin to burn. "What about Riley? Is she okay?"

"They're moving her to the recovery unit where she will wake up from the anesthesia." He pauses, his facial expression stoic. "Her blood pressure is still high, which we are hoping will come down over the next few days. Her kidneys were severely affected by the condition but that is another thing that should resolve since we delivered the baby."

"What happens now?"

"I will take you to the nursery so you can see the baby. Since we will be transferring your wife soon, one of the nurses can take you and the baby to her room."

None of this feels real. "Okay," I tell him, nodding as I pull my phone out to text Nova. The doctor rises to his feet and I follow him out of the room as he leads me away from the surgical unit. I give Nova an update on everything, tucking my phone back into my pocket as I follow him through the postpartum unit.

We round a corner and there's a nursery in the center, surrounded by three glass walls so you can see inside. From what I read, babies go directly to the rooms with their mothers unless there are issues preventing that from happening.

I follow him into the room, looking at the nurses who are moving about, although I don't really see them. The past hour has been a blur, I'm not sure what my brain has really registered because I don't have a single memory of the panic and chaos that has ensued.

The doctor stops as we reach the only bassinet that is occupied in the room. I look down, my heart stumbling over itself as my breath catches in my throat. He's wrapped tightly in a pastel blue blanket with a pink-and-blue striped hat covering his head. My eyes burn as my gaze travels over his perfect little face, his plump lips, and little round nose. His dark lashes rest against the tops of his full cheeks.

"Here's your little guy," the doctor says, the smile evident in his voice as he looks up at me with his eyes shining from the fluorescent lights above. "Congrats, Dad."

CHAPTER TWENTY-SEVEN
ROWAN

This shit is absolutely insane.

And terrifying.

And I can't help but feel bad for my best friend right now.

We're all family, so it's hard to sit back like this, not knowing what's going on, but Nova keeps assuring everyone that they're taking care of Riley. It's hard to believe her, though, when her face says she doesn't even believe herself.

The entire waiting room is silent. Nash is still with the doctor and we have no idea where they took him or what he's doing. Lincoln is sitting next to Nova with his arm around her shoulders, holding her tightly against his side. Carson's sitting next to me, staring down at his phone.

Caleb left ten minutes ago since he had to go relieve his nanny, but we all promised to keep him in the loop.

It's understandable that he had to leave and no one faults him for it.

My eyes scan the room as my mind runs rampant with thoughts. Situations like this make me glad that I've made the clear decision to never settle down. I've never wanted kids for a number of reasons, but mainly because the thought of having someone dependent on you like that terrifies me.

I can barely keep myself together, let alone having to worry about caring for someone else. I can't even imagine what Nash must be going through right now. All I know is, I will never put myself in a position like this.

Settling down? No.

Having kids? Fuck no.

Movement catches my attention from the hall and my stomach almost falls to the floor as I catch sight of her auburn-colored hair.

"Hadley?" I instantly say without even thinking as I climb to my feet. Carson glances up at me, but I ignore him as I start to walk in her direction.

She pauses in the hall, just outside the door, her hazel eyes instantly finding mine. "Rowan? What are you doing here?"

Hadley dated my brother Beau for almost two years, but he went and fucked it all up when he cheated on her last summer. Beau and I don't exactly get along, so I don't blame her for ending things with him, especially after how shitty their break-up was. I haven't seen her since that night, which makes it even weirder seeing her here… four hours from where she calls home.

"I could ask you the same thing."

"I'm here on a traveling contract," she says with simplicity as I step into the hall with her. We move to the side, sure to stay out of anyone's way, although it's quiet in the hospital now. "I've been here for a little over a month, although I'm hoping maybe they'll hire me full-time after my contract is up." She tilts her head to the side. "Now it's your turn."

"A friend's…" I pause, thinking of what the hell Riley even is to Nash. I know he's been staying with her. Tonight he called her his wife. Hell, I have no fucking clue. "Wife?" The word comes out like a question and she gives me a weird look. "Yeah, I don't know the specifics of their relationship, but she had an emergency C-section, and we're just waiting to hear what's going on."

Her nostrils flare. "I think I know who you're talking about."

I nod in understanding, although not completely agreeing with it. "They took Nash, so I think that might be a good sign."

"It is," she says with a small smile. "I'm not legally allowed to say anything because of HIPAA, but it's not a bad sign, if that helps."

Relief instantly floods me. It doesn't mean her situation isn't any less serious, but it definitely brings me some comfort. "Thank you, Hadley. It really does."

"Good," she says, smiling as her hazel eyes shine back at me. "Well, it was nice seeing you and I hope everything goes well with your friend's wife… or whatever she is," she adds with a wink.

"Ro, come here," Carson calls for me, ducking his head through the doorway. "Nash just texted Nova."

"Shit, okay. I'll be right there," I tell him, glancing at him and then back to Hadley. My gaze meets hers in a rush. "Maybe I'll see you around?"

She bites back a grin. "Maybe you will."

I watch as she turns around, her auburn hair swishing in a ponytail as she heads back down the hallway. I wait a moment, shaking away thoughts I shouldn't be having about my brother's ex before dipping back into the waiting room.

CHAPTER TWENTY-EIGHT
NASH

"Do you want to hold him?"

I stare down at the newborn baby in the bassinet, absolutely terrified to even touch him. The only baby I've had experience with was Posey and that was only because Nova wouldn't let me be afraid. She insisted I learn how to hold her and feed her, so I know the basics… but this is different.

Completely different.

My eyes flash to the nurse and I quickly read her name tag before looking back at her. "Am I allowed to?"

"Well, yes," Sabrina laughs softly, sliding one hand under his head and the other under his body. "We encourage the mom and dad to hold them as soon as they are able to. Skin to skin is best, but you can do that when you get back to the room." She effortlessly lifts him from the bassinet, moving closer as she lifts him toward me. "Here you go, Dad."

My eyes widen as I take him from her, not bothering to correct her. My heartbeat is turbulent in my chest. He stirs slightly in his sleep as I tuck him in closer to my body, his head resting along the inside of my elbow. I watch in amazement as his mouth pops open, his jaw stretching as he yawns.

"He's amazing," I muse quietly, not sure whether I'm talking to the nurse or myself. I cradle him in my arms and I feel Sabrina squeeze my shoulder before she walks back over to the nurses' station.

I stand in place, half afraid to move as I stare down at his features. He has Riley's nose. I push his hat back, just enough to see his almost black hair. I spent months wondering what he would look like and now here he is.

"You came a little earlier than expected, bud," I tell him, my voice barely audible. "It's okay, though. You're safer out here now and so is your mom." My heart lurches into my throat at the thought of her. "We need her to be good, buddy. We both need her here with us."

The nurse walks back over to me. "They have a room ready for you guys. I can take you there to wait for your wife."

"Is she okay?"

She nods, her expression giving nothing away. "She's still waking up, but they should be bringing her in, in a little while." She glances at the baby. "Do you guys have a name picked out for him?"

"Not yet," I tell her, thinking back on the handful of

names Riley was stuck on. "We didn't expect him to be here already."

"I'm sure you guys will pick the perfect name for the most handsome little man," she says, her eyes dropping to his face on the last three words. She motions to the bassinet. "Let's get him back in there and I'll show you to your room."

Following her command, I gently lay the baby down, careful to make sure he doesn't wake up. When I held Posey, she was a few days old. This is the first time that I've ever held a baby within their first few hours of life.

Sabrina guides me down the hall, walking along beside me as I push the bassinet. It's quiet in the postpartum unit, and we're tucked away in a corner room. The lights are dim as we step inside, and my throat constricts as I see the empty space where a bed should be. I need to see her. I need to know she's okay with my own two eyes.

"I recommend doing skin to skin, if you feel comfortable. If you take off your shirt and remove his blanket, just place him on your chest, but I would cover him with the blanket so he doesn't get cold." She pauses, pulling a drawer out from the bassinet. "Diapers and wipes are in here. He should be hungry in the next hour or so, so just press the call button when he wakes up and I will bring a bottle by and show you how to feed him.

I stare at her, the overload of information stacking

up in my mind. "Wait. That's it? You're just going to leave him here with me?"

She laughs softly, a smile pulling on her lips. "Yes. Bonding is extremely important and the two of you need that time. You will be okay and if you need anything, just call."

"Uh, okay," I force out the words, feeling less than fucking confident as she disappears from the room, leaving the baby and I alone. I look down at him. "Guess it's just you and me now, little buddy."

Pulling my phone out from my pocket, I take a picture of him sleeping peacefully, sending it to my sister, along with a picture of the little card with his birth info.

NOVA

Oh my gosh, look at him.

NASH

He's perfect.

NOVA

How is Riley?

NASH

She's still in recovery but they should be bringing her to the room sometime soon.

I think it will be best if everyone just sees her another day.

Maybe even after we get home.

The last thing I want to do is bombard Riley with a group of people while she's not feeling well. I know they are family and everyone means well, but she needs time to process. Time to spend with her little boy.

> NOVA
>
> I agree. She needs some time to recover. I just didn't want to leave until we knew what was going on.

> NASH
>
> I get it. I know she'll appreciate knowing everyone was here because I certainly do.

> NOVA
>
> You're a good husband, Nash.

My stomach falls onto the floor. I completely forgot about the scene I made in the waiting room... never mind the fact that I was calling her my wife in front of everyone.

> NASH
>
> I can explain.
>
> It was the easiest way to solve her insurance issues. We got married so she would have access to my medical care.

> NOVA
>
> Do you love her?

My breath hitches.

> NASH
>
> What?

NOVA

Don't you dare play stupid with me, Nash Theodore Simmons. I've spent years watching the way you look at my best friend. You've been living in her house, taking care of her, marrying her to help her, and now you're waiting for her in a hospital room with her baby.

DO. YOU. LOVE. HER?

My heart aches and I stare down at the baby before looking back at my phone.

> NASH
>
> Yes.

NOVA

Good.

You need to tell her, Nash.

> NASH
>
> I know.

NOVA

And then you need to give her a proper wedding.

> NASH
>
> What makes you think she would want that with me?

NOVA

Just trust me. I know my best friend.

> Give that sweet baby a kiss for me and keep me updated.

NASH
> Of course. Love you, sis.

NOVA
> Love you, big brother.

I lock the screen of my phone, tucking it back into my pocket before looking back at the baby. His eyelids slowly peel open and his eyes instantly meet mine. He stares right through me, wonderment filling me as I watch him studying my face. I don't think babies can see that well, but he doesn't look away from me.

"Hey, bud," I murmur as I lean closer to him. "I don't know if you remember me from when you were in your mom's belly, but I'm Nash and I'm hopelessly in love with your mother."

He blinks, his lips parting as he stares back at me with his sleepy eyes.

"I know you don't know what the hell I'm saying, but that's okay." I slide my hands under him, slowly lifting him into my arms as I tuck him close to my body again. "I'm going to be honest and tell you that I don't really know what I'm doing here, so we're just going to have to figure all this out together."

He makes a soft sound and lets out what sounds like a sigh. I watch his face, his lips turning downward as his expression cracks and he lets out a wail.

"Oh shit."

I don't know what the hell I'm supposed to do now.

I glance around the room, attempting to slowly rock him in my arms, shushing him. The call bell is on the remote attached to the wall. My footsteps are slow as I walk to it, bending my knees to pick it up as I press the button.

His cries begin to subside as his eyes begin to search my face again. The door opens behind me and I turn around to find the nurse walking in with a bottle.

"Someone sounds like he's hungry." She smiles, walking over to the two of us. "Come sit and I'll show you what to do," she tells me, motioning to the rocking chair. I walk over, slowly sitting down as I prop him up in my arms. She hands me the bottle, showing me what to do, and takes a step back as she watches me feed him.

He sucks on the nipple, drinking some of the milk, but it doesn't last long before he drinks the amount she wanted him to have and he falls back asleep again. She takes the bottle from me, setting it down on the table. "Good job." She grabs a burp cloth, throwing it over her shoulder. "I'll show you how to burp him and you can do it next time."

I hand him off to her, watching her as she does it, gently bouncing him up and down as she pats his back until he finally burps. "How do I do skin to skin with him?"

Sabrina looks at me, a smile growing on her lips. "Grab that blanket," she says, pointing at the back of the chair. "Take off your shirt and we'll get him on your chest."

She turns away, giving me privacy that I don't care about as I remove my shirt and cover back up with the blanket. She waits until I'm ready, turning back around as she starts to unwrap the cloth around him. I move the blanket from me as she strips him down to his diaper. She holds on to him, positioning his chest and stomach against mine before taking the blanket to cover both of us.

His little body is so warm against me, and I hold him against my chest, making sure he's protected and secure as he sleeps on me. I watch Sabrina as she grabs the remote, stretching the cord so it's sitting on the arm of the chair. She leaves the two of us with the promise of only being a call away.

I slowly begin to rock, my heart growing inside my rib cage as I cradle the baby boy. I don't know how long we stay like that, but an hour easily passes as I stare down at him in wonderment. He truly is amazing. Riley really fucking did it. She grew a whole-ass person in her belly and now here he is.

There's a soft knock on the door. I continue to rock, my head turning to the side as I watch the door open and a bed is wheeled in, with a handful of medical professionals following. I sit up straighter, holding the baby firmly against my chest as they push Riley into the room, setting her bed up in the empty space.

"She woke up in recovery and we waited until she

was stable enough to be moved, but she seems to have fallen back asleep," the one nurse explains to me as she smiles at Riley and then me. "She's pretty exhausted from everything that happened today."

I slowly rise to my feet, keeping the blanket secured around the baby so he isn't exposed to the cool air in the room. My stomach sinks when I see Riley lying in the bed. Her long dark hair is pulled away from her face in a braid and she looks so incredibly pale and fragile.

"Is she okay?"

The nurse nods as she connects her IV tubing to a bag hanging on the pole beside the bed. "Her blood pressure has already started to come down, but we still have to keep her on medication to prevent seizures for at least another day. Her kidney function has begun to improve, so it appears that the injury was acute."

Relief floods me. "So, she's going to be okay."

"Yes." She smiles, the warmth radiating from her expression. She looks over everything once more, making sure Riley is connected to the different monitors and fluids. "I will be back in a little bit to check on her again."

I stare down at Riley as the nurse disappears from the room. Her son stirs against my chest and I hold him close as I lower myself down onto the edge of her bed.

"We're here waiting for you, mama. Whenever you're ready to wake up, we'll be here."

I'll always be here.

CHAPTER TWENTY-NINE

RILEY

The faint sound of voices in the distance becomes a little louder, although I can't make out any of the words they're speaking. My eyelids feel lighter than they did the last time I tried to open them. Peeling them open, I quickly blink as my eyes adjust to the dim lighting while trying to draw my surroundings into focus.

The last thing I remembered after waking up from surgery was being told they were moving me to my room. I was exhausted and so tired that as soon as they wheeled my bed into the hallway, I fell back asleep. Somehow I slept until now—although I'm not entirely sure how much time has passed.

There's a twinge of panic inside of me again as I realize that I'm alone. No Nash. No baby. Just me.

I blink a few more times, my eyes moving from the ceiling and along the walls. My hands slide off my stomach and I plant them at my sides, my entire body feeling weak as I try to scoot up farther in the bed. My legs don't move, considering the fact that I still haven't regained feeling in them and my feet.

A searing pain slices through my abdomen. "Fuck," I mutter, wincing in pain as I suck in a breath. My face screws up and I move my hands back to my stomach, remembering I was cut open only a few short hours ago.

"Riley."

His voice. Oh my god, *his voice*.

I lift my head, turning it to the side as I see him walking toward me without his shirt on. My eyes drift over his torso and I don't even get the chance to ask him as tears immediately spring from my eyes. "Hi."

"We've been waiting for you," he says quietly, coming over to stroke the side of my face. His lips instantly find my forehead, warm and soft against my skin. "You gave us all quite the scare."

"I know," I tell him, my throat burning from the tube that was inserted during the surgery. Nash pulls away from my forehead, his eyes scanning my face as I lift my head farther, attempting to look around. "Where is he?"

The softest smile lifts Nash's lips. "I just laid him down." He moves away from the bed, pushing the small bassinet over to me before he lifts the baby up, bringing him to me. "Do you think you can hold him?"

The medications they have me on to prevent

seizures are still making me feel groggy and the thought of dropping him has me nervous. "Can you help me? Just in case?"

"Of course," he says softly, as he brings the baby down to me, setting him down in my arms. His hands linger, providing additional support for me, just in case I'm too weak.

For the first time since he was born, I see my baby's face—and I crumble.

My chest constricts, my jaw hurting from the overwhelming emotion as I get choked up. He's so perfect. His little nose, his soft cheeks. Tears stream down my cheeks and I trail my fingers over his face, memorizing every single inch of him.

"Oh, Nash," I half sob, blowing out a breath as I continue to stare at the baby. "How is he so perfect?"

"Because he's a piece of you."

My eyes move to Nash's and he stares back at me—the emotion in his expression damn near palpable. His throat bobs as he swallows hard, his hand reaching up to cup my cheek.

"I love you, Riley."

My heart stumbles over itself in my chest, the air leaving my lungs in a rush. "What?"

"You're my home," he says, his voice a tender embrace. "You're my safe space where I can just forget about everything else going on. My heart just knows you and it always has. There has always been something that felt like it was missing and I think it was you. My soul has just been waiting for you."

Tears blur my vision once again as I'm completely overwhelmed with emotion. This entire birthing experience has been nothing like I expected, and I'm sure I'll be dealing with the mental fuck after I am discharged. I'm exhausted and tired, yet happy, but also feeling like I was robbed of the first few hours of my baby's life.

But somehow Nash's words push all of those negative things to the back of my mind.

"Nash." His name comes out like a broken whisper. "I've always loved you, I just never wanted to admit it. I was always so afraid you would never feel the same way about me. I love you so much."

A smile lifts his lips. "I know this is probably terrible timing, all things considered." He pauses, his smile falling. "But I needed you to know. I was so afraid when I talked to Nova after the game, and even more so when I got here."

"I'm sorry about that," I tell him, feeling a twinge of guilt for how everything played out. "I didn't want you to worry about me, so I said I was fine. I knew I wasn't, so I called the doctors and they told me I needed to come in. I thought it was going to be something simple and they would send me home."

"Well, I think it looks more like them sending you home with a baby now."

I stare down at his perfect little face before looking

back at Nash. "What are your plans? You know, after we get out of here."

He looks at me, his eyes burning holes into my soul. "You are my plan, Riley. You and this little guy," he says, his hand reaching for the baby's. "I want both of you."

"Does that mean you'll stay?"

"I'll sell my fucking house if you want me to." He slides his hand to mine. "When I said I love you, I meant that in a 'I want you forever' kind of way." A soft smile drifts across his lips.

"Forever with you sounds nice."

"Good," he says with a smile as he gives my hand the gentlest squeeze. "Because we can't get this marriage annulled since we've had sex."

It never once occurred to me, the stipulations to getting a marriage annulled. Once a marriage is consummated, an annulment is no longer an option. No one would actually know that we've had sex, especially considering the fact that the baby isn't Nash's, but the thought of lying about something like that just feels wrong.

This marriage isn't what it was originally supposed to be. We were never supposed to fall in love, but here we are.

"It's okay," he tells me with a wink as he leans toward me, his lips pressing against my temple. "No one has to know about it at our real wedding."

"Real wedding?" Tears blur my vision yet again.

"This isn't my official proposal. I have better plans for that," he explains, pressing his forehead to mine. "I want all of you. I want all of him. I want all of us," he says with a soft breath. "Will you be mine?"

"Can I tell you a secret?" I ask him, my eyes searching his.

He pulls back slightly, a touch of worry flashing in his irises. "Of course."

"I've always been yours."

"Thank God," he murmurs, letting out a breath as a smile breaks out across his lips before he presses them to mine. He kisses me with a tenderness that has my soul melting inside of my body. It's a closed-mouth kiss, but there's still such an intensity that rocks me to my core.

My god, I love this man.

Nash pulls away from me, his fingers dancing across the baby's face as he looks down at his features. "Have you decided on a name for him?" he asks me, his voice quiet before his eyes meet mine again.

"I think I have," I tell him, my voice equally quiet. "I think he looks like a Theodore." My eyes search his, looking for any type of aversion from him. The past few weeks, I've been thinking about using his middle name as the baby's name, but I wasn't sure how to approach the subject. Now that we've met the little guy, I think it just fits. "Don't you think so too?"

The softest smile dances across his lips, his eyes

shining brightly back at me. "I think it's a perfect name for him," he concurs, the emotion thick in his voice as he looks back down at the baby. "Little Theo." The smile doesn't leave his lips as he looks back at me. "I love you, Riley."

"I love you."

***

The next week flies by in a rush. Between broken sleep, probably a thousand diapers, and countless bottles, I don't even know what day it is when I'm finally discharged from the hospital. My blood pressure ended up stabilizing within two days after my surgery and my kidneys rebounded relatively quickly.

They'll still be monitoring me closely to make sure that everything continues to get better, but as of now, my health is stable enough for me to go home. There's no need for Theo or me to be here any longer, and I am honestly so fucking thrilled.

This entire experience has been a roller coaster and I've already set up therapy appointments, so I can try and work through the trauma before it ends up compounding. All things considered, I feel like I've been managing it pretty well so far.

Then again, I have very little time to actually stop and think about everything that happened.

"Are you ready to go, mama?" Nash asks me as he pokes his head back through the door. He left fifteen minutes ago so he could pull up out front and the nurse could check the car seat.

As I finish adjusting the hat on Theo's head, I look up at him, a smile pulling on my lips. "Let's go home."

The nurse wheels me out to the car and helps us in, me sitting in the back with the baby before they send us on our way. Nash drives probably ten miles per hour under the speed limit the entire way back to my house. As we pull into the driveway, I see a string of blue balloons creating an archway around the front door.

Nova has been dying to come see us and thankfully Nash kept everyone out of the hospital for my sake. I ended up FaceTiming her while we were in there, but it was nice to just have it be the three of us, except for when Nash had to leave for work. He'll be leaving tomorrow night for another away game, but he's already asked Nonna to come stay with me while he's not here.

Nash helps me out of the car before going over to lift the baby out and we begin our walk up to the house. He stands to the side, letting me in, and relief wraps around me as I step into the comfort of my own home. It feels like it's been an eternity since I've been here. I can't wait to get a real shower, change into fresh clothes, and snuggle up on the couch with my boys.

Instead, I just walk directly to the sofa and slowly sit down, careful to support my midsection. It still feels like my insides are going to tumble out of my stomach, but it's more bearable than it was at first. The first time they had me get out of bed was absolute torture. They like to have patients up and moving within six to eight hours after surgery to promote blood flow, but I had to wait two days thanks to my body betraying me.

"It's kind of weird that they just send you on your way with a tiny-ass person like you know what you're doing."

I look over at Nash as he gets a sleeping Theo out of his car seat and holds him against his chest as he walks over to the couch. "You'd think they would give you some instructions or something."

"Right?" he says, raising his eyebrows as he lowers himself down beside me. "Like what do we do now?"

Handing the baby to me, he makes sure he's secure in my arms before he wraps his around the tops of my shoulders. He scoots closer until I'm tucked in against his side. I move my head, resting it against his shoulder as I breathe in the scent of him. "I think we're just supposed to enjoy it."

"I think you might be right." He presses his lips to the top of my head. "I'll spend the rest of my days enjoying my time with the two of you… and however many other babies you let me put in you."

Laughter bubbles in my chest. "You're absolutely insane, you know that, right?"

"Insane about you, mama," he says, his voice tangling around my soul. "Always you."

EPILOGUE
NASH

Six months later

Rocking on the chair, I stare down at Theo, my eyes traveling over the contours of his face as I memorize every single developing feature. I feel like I've taken the time to memorize the way he looks at every single stage, as it feels like he's always growing and showing no signs of slowing down.

If you would have told me a year ago that I'd be completely smitten by a little six-month-old baby, I would have told you, you were insane. He may not be mine biologically, but goddammit, he is mine.

The past six months haven't been easy, but we've made it this far. Things between Riley and me have been absolutely amazing. Better than I could have imagined anything ever being. I ended up listing my place for rent and completely moved in with her and Theo, although I was already living with her anyway. It just was never official. It felt weird having all my things at my old house, and Riley agreed.

She wanted me here permanently with the two of them and considering the fact that she's a permanent fixture inside of my soul, it only made sense.

After we got home and Riley got settled, it was clear the trauma she experienced with Theo's birth was something she needed to deal with. Before she left the hospital, she made an appointment with her therapist and began working through everything immediately. I couldn't personally relate to her because I didn't have the same experience she did, but I knew the only thing I could really do was be here for her and be supportive.

When Riley was having a bad day, I made sure to step in and minimize the things she had to do, whether it was with Theo or just in general. My schedule with hockey made things a bit challenging, but thankfully we have quite the village of people here.

Nonna didn't hesitate to step in when I was away and Nova was constantly checking in on Riley. Riley's always been hardheaded and has struggled to ask for help, but thankfully everyone already knew that. She's the type of person where you just have to tell her that you will be helping her and she usually doesn't put up a fight about it then.

Theo's been asleep for probably ten minutes now, but he's still in my arms as I slowly rock on the chair. His weight feels comfortable in my arms, like this is exactly where he's supposed to be. I watch his little lips curl upwards as he stirs in his sleep, smiling deeply about something.

He's the most amazing thing I've ever experienced, other than the love from his mother.

As I begin to rise from the chair, I hear a noise outside that sounds faintly like a car door shutting. Riley went out with the girls tonight, so it was just Theo and me this evening. I've been enjoying my time at home a little too much and the thought of having to resume the grueling hockey season in the next month or so has me feeling a little disappointed.

I walk over to Theo's crib, slowly lowering him down onto the mattress. He stirs a bit, but he's good at staying asleep. He adjusts on the bed and I grab his blanket, pulling it over his body as he settles. Standing by the railing for another moment, I stare down at him, my heart swelling in my chest at my son.

Making sure his white noise machine is set for the night, I pull the door shut behind me, leaving it cracked open before making my way downstairs. As I'm coming down the steps, I hear the sound of the front door softly closing and Riley curses as her keys clatter onto the floor. She's holding on to the wall, bracing herself with one hand, as she fights with her heels with the other, attempting to unstrap them.

A soft chuckle escapes me as I walk over to her. "Let me help you, love," I tell her, grabbing a small stool for me to sit down on. Riley drops her foot to the floor, her eyes a bit glazed over as she gives me a crooked grin. Bending forward, I reach for her foot, lifting it into the air until she plants her heel on my thighs.

"Thank you," she murmurs, watching me as I unstrap her heel, pulling it away from her foot before moving to the next. Her foot lingers on my legs and I grab her ankle, my fingers slowly trailing up the length of her calf, drifting around her knee before moving up her thigh.

"Did you have fun tonight?"

Riley blows out a soft breath, her hands reaching for my shoulders as she pulls her foot away from my legs. Instead of pulling her into my lap, I stand up, my hands finding her hips.

"I did, but I'm glad to be home now," she breathes, tilting her head back to look up at me. "How was Theo?"

"You know he's always good."

"You're such a good dad." Her smile grows wider, her eyes shining back at me as she stares up at me. "He loves you so much."

"I hope so," I tell her, my hands trailing along her lower back. "I want to be the best version of myself for both of you."

"Well," she starts, her arms linking around the back of my neck, the faint smell of fruit and liquor on her breath. She gently kisses one corner of my mouth before pulling back to look at me. "You're the best father he could ever ask for." She lifts up on her toes, pressing her lips to the other side. "And you're the best husband I could ever ask for."

My cock is already hard because fuck… it's just what she does to me.

"I don't think I'll ever get tired of hearing you call me that."

She tilts her head to the side. "Call you what?"

"Your husband."

She laughs softly, the sound the sweetest melody to my soul. I watch her as she pulls away from me, her hands trailing over my chest, slowly traveling down my torso until she's reaching the hem of my shirt.

"What are you doing, mama?"

"I think it's only right if I show my husband how much I appreciate him," she murmurs, lifting my shirt up before dropping it onto the floor. Her hands reach for the waistband of my pants as she lowers herself down onto her knees.

"Fuck, Riley," I groan as she pulls my cock from my pants, wrapping her hand around the shaft. She looks up at me, her tits practically spilling from the top of her low-cut blouse. Her lips part, her soft breath drifting across the tip before she trails her tongue over it. "I love how my wife looks when she's on her knees for me."

"Yeah?" she says, her voice sultry and thick with need as her tongue darts out and she drags it along the underside of my dick, running the tip along her skin stretched over the barbells. She bats her eyelashes, her bright green eyes staring up at me as she wraps her lips around my cock, slowly sliding it into her mouth.

"Jesus Christ, look at you," I moan, my hand instantly fisting her silky hair as I grip it close to her scalp. She doesn't stop until she's gagging around my length, the muscles in the back of her throat constricting around the tip. "I love how you look with my cock shoved down your throat."

Tears spring to her eyes, but she doesn't release me. Instead, she bobs her head again, pumping her hand around my length as she slides her tongue along the underside of my cock, sucking me in and out. Every now and then, the tip hits the back of her throat, making her gag as she chokes on me. Heat swells in the pit of my stomach and I already feel like I could come from the way she takes me.

I can feel myself getting closer by every second as she continues to suck me harder. My hips involuntarily rock, my grip tightening on her hair before I pull back, pulling her away from me. My cock leaves her lips with a popping sound and her eyes widen as she looks up at me, searching mine with concern as saliva drips from her lips.

"Stand up."

She doesn't argue and I release her hair as she climbs to her feet, her eyes burning holes through mine. "Did I do something wrong?" For a moment, worry crosses her expression and I see she's about to shut down. "I'm sorry. I thought I was doing what you liked, but I don't know. I had a few drinks, so maybe I'm not doing my best."

"Riley." Her name falls from my lips as a command and she stops, staring back at me. "I'm not ready to come and if you keep sucking my dick like that, I'm going to be coming down your throat in the next few seconds." I watch her face relax, her shoulders dropping as I close the distance between us. "I'm not ready to be done with you, and you suck my dick like it's your fucking job."

She bites back a grin, a soft laugh falling from her lips. I bend my knees, my hands sliding down to her thighs as I swiftly lift her into the air, earning a gasp from her as I carry her in my arms. Her legs instinctively wrap around my waist and I feel the warmth from her pussy through the thin material of her panties as her skirt shifts up around her hips.

"Now, where do I go with you?"

I glance around the foyer, contemplating fucking her on the floor before I walk into the kitchen. It's closer than the couch and I want to sink deep inside of her, fucking her into oblivion. I don't stop until we're at the island, and a bag of yogurt snacks falls onto the floor as I set her down. Riley reaches for me, her hands finding the nape of my neck as she pulls me to her.

My lips find hers in an instant, meeting her as she kisses me with an intensity that rocks me to my core.

She's taking everything she wants and I'll never be the one to tell her no. Her tongue sweeps along the seam of my lips and I part them, letting her in as her tongue tangles with mine. My cock is still out and I kick my pants and boxer briefs away so I'm standing completely naked in the kitchen, nestled between her legs as we kiss until we're breathless.

Riley pulls away, her hands finding the hem of her blouse as she strips it away from her body, her full tits falling from the shirt as she tosses it onto the floor.

"No bra?" My eyes find her as I slide my hands over her breasts, pulling on her nipples. "My wife knew she wanted to get fucked as soon as she got home."

"Yes, she did," she murmurs, her eyelids fluttering shut as I twist her nipples. Cupping one breast, my mouth drops down to the other, tasting and teasing the bundle of nerves before moving to the other. Riley withers beneath my touch, pressing against me as she searches for some kind of friction between her legs.

"You're so fucking sexy," I groan, my hands roaming down her torso and stopping as I reach her center. I slide my finger beneath the thin fabric of her panties, hooking it around them as I pull the lace to the side. I slide my fingertip through the moisture. "You're fucking soaked."

"Because of you."

Grabbing my cock with my other hand, I hold her panties to the side as I slide the tip of my cock through her wet lips. Her head tips back, a moan escaping her as

I slide into her, not bothering to remove the rest of her clothing. I just want to be balls deep inside of her, filling her with my cum.

She plants her hands on the counter, her head lifting as her eyes find mine. I grab her hip with one hand, the other moving between her legs as my fingers find her clit. "Fuck." She lets out a loud moan, her face screwing up as I begin to play with her cunt while I slowly fuck her.

"You like that, don't you, mama?" I groan, pistoning my hips as I fuck her a little harder. Shifting my hand, I plant my thumb against her clit, rolling it around, applying more pressure as I slide my cock in and out of her. My eyes drop down between us and I watch the way her cunt stretches around my length, taking every fucking inch.

She's a mess of moans, her head falling back again as I begin to fuck her harder. "Don't stop, Nash."

Her entire body shifts on the counter and I start to fuck her harder and faster. "Hold on to me, Riley," I order, my voice tense as I grip her hip tighter. She's so close, I can feel it already with the way she clenches around me. Riley reaches for me, her hands finding my shoulders. Her nails dig into my flesh as I pin her against the counter, slamming into her over and over again.

My thumb rolls over her clit, my movements rushed as she lets out a string of curses. My name falls from her lips as she falls apart around me, her cunt taking my cock deep inside as she comes. Her orgasm tears through her body and she pulls me down with her. Heat spreads through my body like wildfire and I rock into her, spilling my cum deep inside her pussy.

I begin to slow, releasing every last drop into her as she rides out the high of her orgasm. My movements stop and I let out a deep, shallow breath, my lungs starved for oxygen as I stare down at her. Riley lifts her eyelids, her gaze instantly finding mine.

My face inches closer to hers, my lips brushing against hers. "I just want to fuck you forever. Can we make that a thing?

"I think we can do that." She laughs quietly, her words breathless and filled with lust. "Till death do we part, right?"

"Yes. Fuck yes," I murmur against her lips again. "I love you," I tell her, honesty pouring from my soul. "God, I fucking love you."

"I love you, Nash. It's you and me."

I pull back just enough to look at her face. "And Theo." I pause, a smile drifting across my lips. "And however many other babies you let me put in your belly."

"Well, if you want a bunch, you'd better get to work."

Pulling her off the counter, I hold her in my arms, my cock already getting hard again as it's still inside her. "You don't have to tell me twice."

Riley laughs quietly and I revel in the sound of her,

in the way she smells, and the way she feels in my arms. She stole my heart long ago, and when I realized it was happening, I was already so gone for her.

I've loved Riley Harris for a lifetime and I'll love her for every lifetime that comes.

EXTENDED EPILOGUE
NASH

TWO YEARS LATER

"Bend over for me, love," I murmur as I push Riley forward. I love her like this—willing and ready for whatever I'm about to give her. Her taut body moves in front of me, bending at the waist as she folds in half and plants her hands against the railing of the balcony. I watch as her slender fingers wrap around it as she glances at me over her shoulder, her long dark hair spilling down her back.

"Aren't you worried someone might see us?"

"Nope." I reach for her, my fingers sinking into her silky locks as I wrap them around my fist, gently giving her a tug. "It's too dark and even if they do, I still don't fucking care," I growl, the cock of my tip pressing into her as I dive in deep. "I want to be inside my wife right now and if someone has a problem with it, they can say something about it."

A moan escapes her, her lips parted and chest heaving as I press into her until I'm filling her completely. We're both stripped bare, our evening clothing on the ground around our feet. The warm air drifts from the Mediterranean Sea, carrying the scent of salt as it blows around us.

Although it's dark and we're up on our balcony, it's a full moon and it wouldn't be hard for someone to see us.

"I don't know if we should be doing this here, Nash," Riley says in a hushed voice as she begins to second guess everything. It's the last night of our honeymoon and I want to spend every second buried deep inside of her.

She was a nervous mess leaving Theo at first and she made me wait until after his first birthday before traveling this far from him. He's safe with Nova and Lincoln and we've FaceTimed every single day, multiple times a day.

My grip tightens on her hair as I slide my other hand around the front of her, my fingers slipping between her thighs as I find her clit. Her body instantly jerks, another moan escaping her in a rush.

"Oh god," she breathes, her eyelids slamming shut. "Fuck, that feels so good."

"I'm not your god, baby," I groan, slamming into her again, watching her knuckles turning white as she braces herself against the movement. "But I am your fucking husband."

She's a breathless mess of moans and I have no intention of stopping until we're both coming. It doesn't take long before I feel her cunt clenching around the length of my cock. I instantly abandon her clit, leaning forward as I lower my mouth to her neck.

"Don't come yet." I lean forward and murmur the words in her ear. She groans in protest as I slowly release my grip on her hair. "I'll tell you when you can come."

"You're not playing fair, Nash."

A smirk plays on my lips. "Who ever said I play fair?" Pulling out of her completely, I grab her waist, hauling her away from the railing as I spin her around to face me.

Fire burns in her eyes and she closes the distance between us, wrapping her arms around the back of my neck. My hands descend down her body, stopping as I grip her ass and lift her into the air. A gasp slips from her lips, her eyes widening as I lower her down onto the railing.

Her legs wrap tightly around my waist, pinning me against her as her nails dig into the back of my neck. "I feel like I'm going to fall."

I tighten my grip on her ass, pulling my hips back just enough to slide my cock back inside of her. The barbells on the underside of my dick moves along her insides, massaging her. "Hold on tight, mama," I tell her, the corners of my mouth twitching. "I promise I'll never let you fall."

Riley holds onto me as I balance her on the edge of the railing, her head tipping back as I piston my hips, fucking her harder. Not only could we be caught, but if my grip slips on her, she could easily fall over the edge. Excitement builds with in me as Riley doesn't object, trusting me completely as I fuck her into oblivion.

Her body moves, her legs tightening around my waist as she holds on tightly. I lose myself in her, my cock slamming into her over and over as I push both of us closer to the edge of ecstasy. Riley Simmons is my entire fucking world and I'll do whatever I have to to keep her safe.

Our surroundings fade away and time doesn't exist. It's only the two of us. Riley is a mess of moans, clinging to me with desperation as her orgasm creeps up on her. Her cunt clenches around my cock, her nails digging deeper into my flesh. My balls draw closer to my body as the familiar warmth builds in the pit of my stomach.

"Come for me, love," I groan, burying my face against her neck as I slam into her once more. The warmth spills into my veins, spreading through my body like wildfire as her orgasm erupts, consuming her completely.

My name falls from her lips in rapid succession as she shatters around me. Pulling away from her neck, I stare at her, watching her eyes rolling back into her head as her face screws up. I lower my face to hers, my name rolling off her tongue as my mouth captures hers, desperately needing to feel her everywhere.

Riley kisses me back, lost in her pleasure as she floats through the abyss. I'm right there with her, filling her with my cum as I pump my cock into her relentlessly. My movements slow, my head swimming in the clouds as I slowly pull away from her, my gaze instantly colliding with hers.

Her glazed eyes find mine, her cheeks pink, hair a mess as she stares back at me. "Can you put me down now?" She laughs breathlessly, wiggling in my arms. A loud gasp escapes her as she shifts backwards a bit, but she's still safe. "Okay, I'm definitely about to fall."

I press my lips to hers as I pull her towards me, lifting her away from the railing. "I would never let you," I murmur against her mouth, her legs falling away from my waist as her feet move back to the ground.

She's a little shaky on her legs, her thighs quivering as she laughs again. "Well, that was something new," she says with a wink. "I think I like this spontaneous side of my husband."

My heart swells as those two last words linger in the air between us. I close the short amount of distance between us, my hands finding her hips again as I pull her flush against me. "Say it again."

She tilts her head back, her chin lifting upwards as

her bright eyes stare through mine, directly into my soul. "*My* husband."

"Goddamn," I breathe, a soft laugh escaping me as I shake my head at her. "I don't think I'll ever grow tired of hearing you say that." She lifts her arms to link them around the back of my neck again. "I don't know what the hell I did to end up with you as my wife."

"Well, for starters, you have excellent insurance benefits." Her face cracks and the sound of her laughter lights my soul on fire. "I'm kidding—but really, that is what started all of this."

"You know, I think I need to thank your old insurance company for sucking so badly," I tell her, clicking my tongue as I tilt my head to the side. Mischief dances along her expression. "Should I send them a basket of fruits? Or perhaps you could make them a nice flower arrangement as a thank you."

Riley pulls me closer to her, laughter escaping her once more. "You're absolutely insane, Nash Simmons."

My lips find hers, feeling the softness of her breath against my flesh. "Insane for you, Riley," I breathe against her mouth as I nip at her full bottom lip. "Only and always for you."

A LOOK INSIDE THE NEXT BOOK

Flip the page for a look inside the next book in the
Aston Archers series coming Spring 2025

PROLOGUE
ROWAN

ONE YEAR AGO

I hate coming back home.

It's not that I don't like my hometown—it's more what comes along with it. It can never be a peaceful visit. Instead, it's always filled with drama of some sort. My parents typically end up arguing about something minute and my brother is a fucking loose cannon. My sister doesn't even like to come back anymore and with how goddamn exhausting it is here, I'm not so sure I blame her.

Raven left as soon as she turned 18 and I was right behind her two years later. The two of us went on to play hockey professionally and Raven was now an assistant coach for the Bears. Our parents tried to get Beau to play hockey at a young age, but he was never really into it. He has always had his own agenda with everything he does and Beau Taylor lives life by the seat of his pants.

He's four years younger than me, six years younger than Raven and he's always been a wild card. He hit the mental illness branch of the family tree and put our parents through hell in high school. His lows can be so goddamn low and his highs frighteningly high, sometimes you aren't so sure he's going to come down.

When he's compliant with his medications, like he has been the past few years, life with him isn't so bad. He can be an abrasive asshole, but he's present in the moment. You can hold a conversation with him without him going on a tangent or freaking out about something. By the skin of his teeth, he managed to graduate college and moved into his own apartment fifteen minutes from our hometown.

"I love this new vase you made," my mother says, setting the piece of pottery down on the center of the table. "Have you heard from your brother at all?"

I glance at my mom as I finish drying a dish and set it down on the counter beneath the cabinet it's supposed to go in. Something resembling dread rolls in the pit of my stomach. "No. I texted him when I was boarding my plane but he didn't respond." Which also wasn't uncommon from him. "I figured he was just coming tomorrow morning."

Beau and I aren't exactly close and we never really were. It's not easy to have a relationship with someone who doesn't fucking like you. He's always had a chip

PROLOGUE

on his shoulder towards Raven and I, making his dislike of us known. When we were growing up, he always blamed us for everything and played the victim, refusing to take responsibility for the fucked up things he's done.

I tried to help my brother, but he just kept pushing back. At some point, you get tired of bailing someone out who would never extend the same favor to you.

It's been a few years since all three Taylor kids were home for Christmas and I can't help but feeling jealous of Rae for being the one who gets the free pass to not show. Last year, she was sick. This year, she's blaming it on work.

She's not the only one who works for a professional hockey team. I know her excuses are bullshit, but I don't call her out on it.

"Beau said he was going to come by tonight. He finally wanted us to officially meet his girlfriend."

How he ended up with Hadley Reed is still a mystery to me. She grew up in the same town as us, although she's two years younger than me, so the two of us were never close. I know her well enough to know she's a seemingly good person. Beau and her started dating about six months ago and it seems like she's been helping to keep him on the straight and narrow.

"When was the last time you talked to him?"

My mother opens her phone, tapping on the screen as her brow furrows. "I talked to him at 10:30," she says, her eyes lifting back to mine as she locks the screen and sets it down on the counter. "He said they would be over after dinner, but it's almost nine now. I would have imagined they'd be here sooner."

I watch her as she picks up her phone, unlocking the screen once again before she scrolls through her phone. She taps on it, lifting it up to her ear as she tries to call him. I can hear it through the speaker pressed to the side of her face as it immediately goes to voicemail. "Did you try calling him earlier?"

"I did," she nods, worry invading her blue irises. "His phone was still on then, but it seems like he's turned it off." I know she's concerned and it's hard not to be, although none of this is uncommon for my brother. Beau has disappeared for months at a time while off his meds and lost in a bottle of alcohol. "He's been doing so well, Rowan."

"I know, Mom," I tell her, my voice soft as my heart breaks for my mother. It's easier for me to have a hard exterior towards my brother. I'm not the one who gave birth to him and raised him. I was merely a bystander in Beau's shit show of a life. "I'll drive by his house and see what's going on."

Her expression is unreadable, but I don't miss the appreciation in her eyes. "Thank you, hon," she says quietly, her lips pursing as she reaches for me, her hand squeezing mine. "Take my car."

"I'll be back in a little bit," I tell her, nodding as a mix of emotions sweeps through me. Sadness for my mother and a myriad of things towards Beau. For once

PROLOGUE

—just one fucking time—could he make this woman's life a little easier?

I head out into the garage, climbing into the sedan before pressing the button to lift the garage door open. As I ease out into the driveway, I pull out my phone, opening up my messages as I tap on my sister's name.

> ROWAN
>
> Be glad you didn't come home again.

RAVEN

What did Beau do now?

You know what, I don't even want to know.

> ROWAN
>
> Just do me a favor and remind me to be busy next year.

RAVEN

Deal.

Tucking my phone back in my pocket, I head in the direction of my brother's apartment, trying to ignore the nagging dread rolling in my stomach. This isn't like the last time. Beau's phone died and time slipped away from him. He didn't decide to go off his meds again and joyride across the country while drinking himself into a stupor and maxing out credit cards.

I push the memories away, focusing on the road for the next thirteen minutes while chewing on the inside of my cheek until it's raw. I faintly taste blood as I pull up along the curb out front, an exaggerated sigh

PROLOGUE

escaping me as I put the car in park and kill the engine. My footsteps are heavy, yet rushed as I stride to the front door.

It's supposed to be shut and locked, but it's open ajar and I slip inside, not stopping until I reach the elevator. He lives on the fourth floor and the car is beginning its descent down to the lobby. As the doors slide open, I see it's open and I head up to Beau's floor, my heart pounding erratically in my chest. It feels like the longest ride of my life.

I head out into the hallway and there's a loud bang echoing throughout the building. I glance around the common area, glancing between the three apartment doors, as if I'm waiting to hear the sound again, trying to figure out where it was coming from. It doesn't take rocket science to figure out it came from the middle one. 402. My brother's apartment.

The door flies open and a flurry of auburn hair comes whipping out as she slams it shut behind her. She doesn't see me at first, tears streaking down the sides of her face as she tucks her chin in against her chest. I'm silent as I watch her, assessing the moment as her chest heaves. She sucks in a deep breath, exhaling slowly as she wipes the tears away from her cheeks.

Her chin lifts, her eyes widening as she sees me standing a few feet in front of her. "Rowan?"

"Is everything okay?"

Her nostrils flare, her bottom lip quivering before a harsh laugh escapes her. "It depends on who you ask."

PROLOGUE

She wipes at her nose, shaking her head as she pushes away from the door. "Your brother seems to be doing just fine."

My eyebrows tug downward, a crease forming between them as I corkscrew my lips. I'm so goddamn confused, I don't even know what piece of this puzzle to touch first. "He's okay?"

"Oh, he's great," she says, waving her hand as pain washes over her irises. "He's getting ready to head to the airport."

Confusion only grows within me as the door behind her opens. Hadley jumps towards me, her body practically colliding into mine as she moves away at lightning speed. My hands instinctively wrap around her biceps, my gaze meeting my brother's over top of Hadley's head.

Beau narrows his eyes as a cruel smirk lifts the corners of his lips. "Well, this is cute. Look at you cleaning up after me." His behavior isn't shocking and it's a sure indicator that he has in fact fallen off the wagon. "One man's trash is another man's treasure."

"Watch it, Beau," I warn him, a bite in my tone as I push Hadley behind me. "You may be my brother, but I won't hesitate to put you on your ass if you keep saying stupid shit."

"Ooh," he half sneers, lifting his hands as he makes them look like he's trembling. "I'm shaking in my boots." He rolls his eyes, pulling his door shut behind him as he looks around me at Hadley. "He's the better pick anyways." Beau moves past the two of us, walking directly to the elevator.

"Where are you going?" I question him, my feet moving as I step up behind him. I hate that this is the relationship I have with my brother. I've always hated it. "Are you off your meds again?"

He lets out a heavy breath. "Jesus Christ, you sound just like everyone else." He spins on his heel, his gaze like a laser point on mine. He doesn't answer my question and that's the confirmation I need. "I can live my life however the hell I want, Rowan."

"I don't give a fuck how you live your life, Beau. I'm here for Mom, not for you and definitely not for me," I tell him, my tone clipped as I cross my arms over my chest. "You told her you were coming after dinner and then your phone was off and she was worried."

"And she just had to send her star son to come check on the degenerate." He lets out another harsh laugh, the sound like sandpaper against my eardrums. "I'm fine, Rowan. I'll call Mom on my way to the airport so she can hear it from me." He sets his jaw, shoving his foot between the elevator doors. "Is that good enough for you?"

My nostrils flare as I stare back at Beau. "Perfect."

Beau doesn't give either of us a second glance or another word as he steps into the car, the doors shutting behind him. The silence hangs heavily in the air and I let out a frustrated breath as I'm acutely aware of Hadley standing behind me.

PROLOGUE

"I know he's your brother, but he's an asshole."

I slowly turn around, a ghost of a smile dancing across my lips. "I use the term brother loosely for him." My eyes scan her face, seeing the conflict written all over her expression. "Where is he going?"

"He said there's nothing here for him in this town. Someone named Darcy said he can come stay with her in Boston. He basically thanked me for my time and told me ours was up."

Boston? Darcy?

I have no fucking clue who she is or what could possibly be there to make him throw everything away like this. Unfortunately, this is Beau. This is what Beau does.

And no one can stop him from doing what he wants.

"I don't know how I could have been so stupid." She shakes her head, her gaze dropping down to her feet. "He knows how to be charming and I fell for the charade like a fucking idiot."

I can't help myself as I step towards her. My forefinger slides under her chin, tipping her head back to look up at me. "Hey, no, stop," I tell her, my voice soft as I lift my other hand to brush away her tears. "This is what Beau does. He uses people and then when they've served their purpose, he discards them like trash."

Anger runs through my veins. This isn't the first time Beau has broken someone's heart and it's not the first time I've had to explain to them that it's not them.

"He has issues—a lot of fucking issues—and not a

single one is your fault or has anything to do with you." I swallow roughly, the painful reminder lodging itself in my throat. "Not everyone is a problem you can fix. You can't help someone who doesn't want to help themselves."

Hadley stares up at me, hope shimmering behind the pain in her chocolate brown irises. "Thank you for saying that, Rowan," she practically whispers, a soft smile cresting her lips. "He was very forthcoming about his struggles with bipolar disorder and something in me thought I could help him." She pauses, letting out an exhale. "It's just reassuring to hear it from someone else."

"Do you want my advice?"

She pulls in her bottom lip, biting down as she nods. "Please."

"You leave all of this in your past. You forget about Beau, you heal and you move on." My tongue darting out to wet my lips, her gaze dropping down to my mouth before bouncing back to my eyes. "And you do not look back."

"You're right," she agrees, confidence washing over her expression as she pushes her shoulders back, straightening my spine. "He was not the one for me. He was just a lesson for me to learn."

I can't help the guilt that floods me. My brother should come with a warning label for anyone who crosses his path. I hope one day he can find happiness and something to settle his soul, but it's not something

PROLOGUE

he was ever going to find in Hadley Reed. She's too good for someone like him.

"Come on," I say softly, my hand dropping away from her as I motion towards the elevator. "I'll walk you out."

She's quiet and I give her the silence as we ride down to the lobby. She collects herself, zipping up her coat as we walk through the foyer to the front door. Her eyes meet mine, a smile on her lips as I hold open the door for her.

"Thanks again, Rowan," she says, nodding at me as we stop in front of the building. "I know you didn't want to come check on him, but I'm glad I ran into you."

I stare at her, my tongue tangling as I stare down at her. My brother's an idiot—a goddamn fucking fool. He was never deserving of someone like her. "Me too."

"Merry Christmas," she tells me, spinning on her heel as she begins to walk away. She gets ten feet away before I start walking after her.

"Hey, Hadley?" I call out, the cool breeze carrying her name with it.

She slowly turns around, her nose already red and her cheeks pink. "Yeah?"

My phone is already in my hand, a new message opened as I hand it to her. "Send yourself a text from my phone."

She takes it from me with hesitation, her eyes dropping to the screen as she types in her number and sends my name in a text to herself. She hands it back to me, her gaze colliding with mine as she tilts her head to the side, her lips parting with a question lingering on her tongue, but she doesn't say anything.

"If you ever find yourself in Aston, let me know," I tell her, tucking my phone into my pocket.

A gentle smile drifts across her lips. "Okay."

"Goodnight, Hadley Reed."

Her eyes shine brightly under the moon, hues of brown and gold swirling together. "Goodnight, Rowan Taylor."

ABOUT THE AUTHOR

Cali Melle is a USA Today Bestselling Author who writes sports romance that will pull at your heartstrings. You can always expect her stories to come fully equipped with heartthrobs and a happy ending, along with some steamy scenes.

In her free time, Cali can usually be found living in a magical, fantasy world with the newest book or fanfic she's reading or freezing at the ice rink while she watches her kids play hockey.

ALSO BY CALI MELLE

ASTON ARCHERS SERIES

Make Your Move

Make Your Play

ORCHID CITY SERIES

Meet Me in the Penalty Box

The Tides Between Us

Written In Ice

Dirty Pucking Play

The Lie of Us

WYNCOTE WOLVES SERIES

Cross Checked Hearts

Deflected Hearts

Playing Offsides

The Faceoff

The Goalie Who Stole Christmas

Splintered Ice

Coast to Coast

Off-Ice Collision

STANDALONES

The Christmas Exchange

The Christmas Rebound

Tell Me How You Hate Me

The Art of Breathing